Books by the same author

Juggling Lessons
Dog on a Broomstick
Dognapped
The Chocolate Monster
It's Not Funny

DRUMMER

JAN PAGE

WALKER BOOKS
AND SUBSIDIARIES

LONDON • BOSTON • SYDNEY • AUCKLAND

This is a work of fiction. Names, characters, places and incidents are either the product of the author's imagination or, if real, are used fictitiously.

First published 2004 by Walker Books Ltd
87 Vauxhall Walk, London SE11 5HJ

2 4 6 8 10 9 7 5 3 1

Text © 2004 Jan Page
Cover photograph © Getty Images/Dieter Steinbach

This book has been typeset in Sabon

Printed and bound in Great Britain by Bookmarque Ltd, Croydon, Surrey

British Library Cataloguing in Publication Data:
a catalogue record for this book
is available from the British Library

ISBN 1-84428-653-3

www.walkerbooks.co.uk

For Adam

press play ▶

1

It was Saturday afternoon and we were hanging around the steps outside the library. A few skaters were showing off their ollies and one-eighties, the Goths were comparing their latest face piercings and a bunch of Kevs were giving us the evil eye from the other side of the square. My skateboard had been run over by a bus so I was freezing my butt off sitting on the concrete, people-watching. There were girls in tight jeans and high heels holding designer carrier bags, enthusiastic families wearing puffy jackets and trooping off to the museum, and elderly couples waddling into the library with their books. Daz was telling me the plot of some film I wasn't interested in and CJ was having a heavy conversation with his soon-to-be-ex-girlfriend, Gemma. As for the weather – well, like CJ, it didn't want to commit itself. If you looked towards McDonald's you'd think it was about to rain, whereas the sky behind the library was a bright plastic blue. The fountain was dribbling into a pool of soggy litter and, according to the broken clock on the museum tower, it was eternally ten past two. I felt as if we were all stuck in a time loop, condemned to repeat the same actions, the same banal conversations, weekend after weekend. And then it happened.

A thought came to me – just popped into my head out of nowhere. It was as if some invisible person had sidled up the library steps and whispered it in my ear. The idea seeped through my brain and into my limbs, dragging me reluctantly to my feet. After four years of responding to every suggestion with "can't be both-ered", I was suddenly full of energy and enthusiasm. Something or somebody was commanding me to act and I had no choice but to obey. I know it sounds ridiculous but, believe me, compared to the weird stuff that happened later it barely registers on the scale. Now I'm sure that strange forces were at work that Saturday afternoon – wheels were turning, as an old friend of mine would say.

Anyway, before I knew what I was doing, I turned to Daz and CJ and said, "Do you want to be in my band?"

"What the hell are you talking about?" replied Daz, raising his eyebrows in disbelief. He knew I'd never had the slightest inclination to form a band – it involved far too much effort and organization. When anyone asked me what I wanted to do when I grew up I'd always said, "As little as possible."

"Yeah, since when have you been interested in music?" added CJ scornfully.

"Always!"

"In listening, maybe. But not playing."

CJ was right. Apart from a couple of terms of learning

recorder, I'd never picked up a musical instrument in my life. Actually, I don't think the recorder even counts as an instrument. It certainly doesn't sound like one – not when I play it, anyway.

"I'll teach myself something," I persisted. "Anyway, Daz, you can play piano, can't you?"

"Not really. I gave up after I failed Grade Two."

"But you could pick it up again, I bet."

We sat in silence for a few moments. On the other side of the fountain Gemma was being comforted by a posse of friends, oozing a girlie mixture of sympathy and outrage. Several indignant looks were thrown in our general direction as they excitedly texted their friends with the tragic news.

"Jason's got a guitar," said CJ thoughtfully. "Pestered the life out of Mum to buy it for him and then gave it up after a few weeks. It made his fingers hurt." Jason was CJ's older brother.

"Jason'll let you borrow it, no problem," I said confidently. "See? We've already got guitar and keyboards."

"So what are you going to play, Liam?" Daz asked.

"Drums," I replied before I'd even had a chance to think. It was as if the decision had already been made for me. "I'm going to be the drummer."

The words reverberated in my head, my brain starting to buzz with possibilities. Suddenly, the library steps stretched out beyond the square, taking me out of the town and into a fantasy world where my band was playing in a vast open-air arena. I could already hear thousands of people clapping and stamping their feet, chanting, begging, pleading for us to come on stage. I could feel the rush of adrenaline as I stepped out and took my place behind a massive, shining drum kit...

"So where are we going to practise?" interrupted the ever-practical Daz.

"I don't know," I mumbled. "In my bedroom."

"But you haven't got any drums."

"I'm sure I can get hold of a kit from somewhere," I said lightly. "Let's not get bogged down with the problems. We've got to be positive. The first thing to do is decide on a name."

So that's how Salamander was born, without any warning, one ordinary Saturday afternoon outside the library – Daz, CJ and me. Of course, I had no idea at the time, but I was about to set out on an extraordinary, involuntary journey that would turn my life upside down and inside out. It would take me well beyond the universe, and yet I'd never be more than a few miles from home. All my previous notions of what was real and possible were going to be discarded along the way – like bits of rubbish tossed from a speeding car. But it was a very long trip, and this was just the key turning the ignition...

2

We took the bus back to Madeley Heath and went our separate ways, but not before arranging to meet up at Daz's place after tea for our first official band meeting. I skipped over a mound of shattered glass on the pavement, danced expertly round the piles of dog mess and took the short cut through the alley to Meadow Walk. This was my street, a short curve of Sixties council houses that looked like something I had made in Design Technology – in other words, badly designed, carelessly constructed and already falling apart. Our house stood at the very centre of this misnamed cul-de-sac and was forever being cursed by angry drivers reversing their cars. Meadow Walk was a dead end in every way, but that evening I felt as if I'd finally found the way out. Onwards and upwards, that was where I was going. I knew it could be years before the band was successful enough for me to physically move out, but mentally I was already packing my bags.

The moment I got through the front door I asked Mum if Salamander could practise in my bedroom. It was not my best piece of timing. She was wrestling with an iced-up freezer drawer, cursing as hundreds of frozen peas cascaded onto the kitchen floor.

"No way, Liam!" Four fish fingers slid out of their box and made a bid for freedom under the kitchen table. Mum snatched them up and then dropped them instantly, her fingers burning with their icy hardness. "Pass us the dustpan and brush, will you?"

"We'll only play when you go out," I offered generously.

"Oh yeah? And how often is that? Once in a blue bloody moon?" It had to be admitted Mum didn't have what you might call a social life. Dad spent most afternoons in the pub, so when it came to the evening he just wanted to collapse in front of the telly. Garry Condie was a lazy slob and he didn't even have teenage hormones for an excuse.

"But you go out every day to work," I reminded Mum, hopping enthusiastically between the sink and washing machine like a small boy.

"Which is when you're at college, isn't it? At least, you're supposed to be."

"It won't be much louder than having the radio on."

"Have you ever played a drum kit, Liam?"

"Not yet, but I'm sure—"

"Have you any idea just how loud it is? It'll take over the whole house. Then your guitarists and your keyboard player will start and nobody will be able to hear themselves, so you'll keep turning the amps up. Before I know it the neighbours will start complaining and I'll have the police round. No!"

"We'll play quietly."

"Oh, don't be so stupid. What rock band ever played quietly? The answer's no, Liam. And don't try asking your dad, either. He won't hear of you being in a band."

"Why not?"

"He just won't, that's all. Please, don't even mention it to him." She gave me one of her funny looks, a cross between a threat and a helpful warning. Not that I had any intention of talking to him about my great plans – to say Dad and I didn't get on was an understatement. I had lost what little respect I ever had for him when he slapped Mum around the face on their wedding anniversary. Since then we'd hardly spoken and we tried not to be in the house at the same time.

I gave up on my mission and watched the football results. Then we had fish fingers and peas for tea – I had a nasty feeling they were the same ones I'd seen Mum sweep up half an hour earlier, but I guessed she wasn't in the mood for complaints about her standards of hygiene. Dad had been in the Grenadier since opening time, and Mum'd had to struggle round the supermarket with my kid sister. Zoe, who had worked her way through the Terrible Twos, the Threatening Threes and was currently in the middle of the Foul Fours, had thrown a tantrum at the sweet shelves when Mum refused to buy a bumper bag of lollipops. Poor Mum, I felt sorry for her. She was only thirty-three, but sometimes she looked about fifty.

It was nearly seven before Dad made an appearance. We froze for a second as we heard the key turn in the lock. The front door swung open and a blast of bad mood and vinegar swept through the hallway. He marched past the lounge and into the kitchen, without bothering to say hello. We heard him flick open a can of beer and unwrap his chip paper.

"I'm going round to Daz's, OK?" I whispered to Mum, rising from the sofa. She nodded.

I crept out of the room and was squeezing open the front door as quietly as I could when Zoe shouted out "Bye, Liam!" at the top of her voice.

"Come here!" Dad barked from the kitchen table. I heaved a huge sigh and trudged back down the hallway.

"What?" I grunted. He didn't look up at me. I watched as he smothered his chips with tomato sauce. Then he took a large swig of beer and put the can down on the table with a deliberate thump. A foamy moustache settled on his top lip. It was obvious that he didn't have anything in particular to say to me; he just liked making me wait. "Well – what?" I repeated.

"What time did you get in last night?"

"Dunno. Late."

"Where did you go?"

"Just to a gig."

"A gig?" he repeated bitterly. "How come you can afford to go to gigs?"

"It was only three quid!"

"Mum give you the money, did she?"

I shrugged.

"Are you still giving him pocket money, Shez?" he shouted into the lounge.

The game show on telly obligingly reached a climax of cheers and applause. But he already knew the answer. Mum gave me bits of money when she had it and always with a health warning: Don't tell your dad. He wiped his mouth and leant back on his chair, his legs wide apart. He wasn't fat, but I could see the beginnings of a beer gut forming itself beneath his white T-shirt. His brown hair was cut close to his scalp, revealing large ears whose lobes were stuck to the side of his head. His neck was thickening up and his features had settled into a permanent scowl. Only his bright blue eyes gave any clue as to why Mum must have once found him attractive. He was wearing shiny navy jogging bottoms and white trainers but, as far as I knew, he'd never run in his life.

He looked me up and down with his usual frown of disgust. "When you going to get yourself a job, Liam?"

"When you get one," I replied instantly. It was a bad move. Dad swore, reached for the nearest weapon – this time, the tomato sauce – and hurled it at my head. I ducked as the bottle smashed into the kitchen unit. Mum ran into the hallway and let out a single scream as she saw me crouching in the doorway. There was ketchup on my hair and face, and splashes of sauce across my T-shirt. Broken glass smeared with red was scattered across the lino. I must have looked like the victim of a bottle fight.

"It's all right," I mumbled. "I'm not hurt." Zoe, dressed in her too-small pyjamas, was hiding behind Mum's legs. She peered out, took one look at the grisly scene and began to howl.

"Shut up!" Dad screamed. He picked up his can and swallowed the rest of the beer in a single gulp. Mum lifted Zoe onto her hip and turned to Dad.

"What did you have to go and do that for?"

"Ask him!" He picked up the remains of his chips and pushed past us, stomping into the lounge with a slam of the glass door. The rest of the house shook as if it was held together with sticky tape. Mum wiped Zoe's tears with a piece of kitchen towel and sat her on the hallway carpet with strict instructions not to move an inch. Then she started picking up the broken shards of glass. She was trying to act calmly for Zoe's sake, but I could see her hands trembling, her eyes filling with tears.

"Don't do it with your fingers," I said. "I'll get a brush."

"You better go out, Liam, or there'll be more trouble."

"But I want to help you clear up."

"Don't worry, love. I'd rather do it myself."

"Sorry…"

"What happened? You didn't tell him about the band idea, did you?" she hissed.

"No, course I didn't."

"You'd better go out now, leave him to calm down."

Mum was right. If I stayed things might get even worse. So I grabbed my hoodie and left the house.

I walked round the corner and took the all-too-familiar route to Daz's block of flats on the edge of the estate. It was dark and Dad's outburst had left me feeling nervous. So I avoided the short cut where gangs of Kevs hung about, waiting to tax anyone whose hair reached below their ears. I stuck my hands in my pockets and put my head down, walking briskly, but not hurriedly, past the row of boarded-up shops and across the car park of the Grenadier.

CJ was already there, his long legs sprawled all over the carpet while he played some beat-'em-up game on Daz's second-hand PlayStation. CJ was tall and slim with high cheekbones; his features were small and even – you could almost call him pretty. He had clear blue eyes and a soft mouth and was dead popular with all the girls. Odd strands of his fair, wavy hair stuck out from under his beanie, a woolly, stripy thing that he'd nicked off Gemma some weeks ago and had no intention of returning. He was wearing a denim jacket covered in badges and the traditional torn baggy jeans. In contrast, Daz was small and scrawny, covered in pale freckles that looked as if they'd been spattered all over his body with a paintbrush. His hair, also down to his shoulders, was thin and mousy. Daz looked permanently off-colour, as if he was sickening for some terrible illness. His hands were dry and papery, bony wrists poking out from the frayed edges of the navy jumper that he wore day in, day out. Daz was always proudly telling us that it had only cost him 30p in the charity shop – it wasn't difficult to see why.

"So, how's it going?" I asked.

"I'm on level five," said CJ.

"I meant the band."

Daz put me in the picture. The situation was not good. Daz couldn't get his keyboard to work and Jason had said CJ could only use his guitar if he paid him rental.

"And Mum said no to us rehearsing at my place," I reported glumly.

"Surprise, surprise," muttered CJ, as his hero was pushed over a precipice with a bloodcurdling scream.

"Let's not bother," said Daz.

"We can't give up that easily!" I cried. "Salamander's only existed since half past three this afternoon!"

"There's only one thing for it, then," said CJ, reaching into a large pocket in the leg of his jeans and taking out his mobile. "I'm calling Gemma."

"Now is not the time to sort out your love life!" I shouted. "We're in the middle of a band meeting, in case you haven't noticed!"

"But I need to get back with her."

"Why? You said she was a stuck-up cow," remarked Daz.

"Yeah, but her kid brother's got a drum kit and she's got a bloody enormous piano in her lounge."

"CJ, you're a genius!" I said, or words to that effect. If I was the creative force behind the band, then CJ was definitely the brains. Daz's contribution was yet to be discovered, but it was early days. We ran down to the Outdoor and bought a massive slab of chocolate and a can of Stella to celebrate. Things were looking up.

3

You had to admire CJ when it came to dealing with girls. Daz and I had listened in awe as he grovelled to Gemma on his mobile last night. He told her that he'd made a terrible mistake, that he missed her like crazy, just couldn't live without her and, by the way, was it all right if he dropped by her house tomorrow with a couple of mates?

"Bloody hell, CJ," I said. "Are you sure you've got the right place?" He had led us right through the town centre and out the other side to Seven Ways, where the seriously rich people lived.

"Yeah, she texted me the address," he insisted, pulling his beanie firmly over his ears as if to block out any further criticism. It was a Sunday afternoon, late September. There were no clouds and the sun was low in the sky. We were tramping along a neat gravel path that took us across the common. There wasn't a scrap of graffiti or a piece of litter in sight. Two little girls were laughing as their father effortlessly tossed a kite into the air and made it soar in the sky. A group of young boys, their bikes strewn casually on the grass, were playing football at the lower end. We passed several elderly dog-walkers who glanced at us suspiciously, as if we were visitors from another world. In a way, we were.

We took a left and found ourselves in the Drive, a wide, leafy street lined with huge detached houses. They had sweeping driveways and large iron gates. Daz counted six Range Rovers parked in front of glossy double garages.

"Does Gemma know you live on the Madeley?" I asked CJ.

"Yeah … sort of."

"So how come she's hanging around with you?"

"I'm her bit of rough," he grinned. Gemma had met CJ a couple of months ago on the library steps. There was a small crowd from the private school that liked to hang out by the fountain, thinking they were full of street cred with their designer skater wear and expensive boards that Mummy and Daddy had bought them for Christmas. Gemma couldn't fail to spot CJ's good looks and had made a beeline for him, probably just to impress her friends. I'd never seen the two of them manage a proper conversation. She used to sit and play with her phone while he skated or talked with his mates. After a while, he'd grab her hand and they'd wander off for a grope somewhere – at least, we guessed that was what they were up to because he always came back with a smile on his face. I don't think they ever went out anywhere together, and CJ had definitely never been invited round for tea.

We walked up the neatly paved **path of** Cedar House. Nobody who lived in the Drive **would** stoop so low as to have a number. I was half expecting a sign in the porch window: *No free newspapers, no double-glazing salesmen, no kids off the council estate.*

Gemma opened the door and immediately threw her arms around CJ's neck, planting a kiss on his cheek. She was wearing dark, studded jeans and a tight red top that revealed a narrow strip of flat stomach, the skin smooth and tanned with a perfectly shaped belly button. I tried my best to look at her face instead. She had brown eyes, a small neat mouth and didn't appear to be wearing any make-up, except perhaps lipstick. Anyone being critical might have said that Gemma had a big nose, but that depended on whether you looked at her from the side or straight on. Either way, she could certainly match CJ in terms of looks – I couldn't understand why he had dumped her in the first place.

"You're ever so late!" she gasped, but it was just a comment, not a criticism. "Cool," she added admiringly. "I didn't know you played guitar."

"It's my brother's," said CJ. "He's, er, lent it to me."

Daz and I mumbled a greeting as we trooped into the massive hallway. There were proper paintings on the wall, a huge chandelier hung from the high ceiling and there were five doors leading, no doubt, to equally grand rooms. An old grandfather clock struck the half-hour, making the three of us jump nervously.

"You on your own?" asked CJ.

"Yes. Mum and Dad have gone blackberrying."

I couldn't help but laugh out loud. I suddenly had this

vision of my own parents in wellington boots and green jackets tramping about with little plastic bowls. Right now Dad would be dozing off in front of the football with a can of lager in one hand and a fag in the other. As for Mum, she was probably still cleaning the tomato ketchup off the kitchen cabinets, dreaming about buying a new fridge-freezer on interest-free credit.

Gemma showed us into what she called "the music room". That was another giggle I had to stifle. A huge grand piano took up most of the space, and sheets of music were piled up on a worn leather armchair. One wall was lined with books and there were family photos all over the piano top. But my eyes settled on the drum kit in the corner. I was itching to have a go but, as CJ hadn't yet told Gemma that this was Salamander's new practice venue, I reckoned I'd better not jump in feet first.

"Where's your brother, what's-his-name?" asked CJ.

"Benedict? Oh, he's at school." We looked at each other blankly. It was Sunday wasn't it?

"He's a boarder," Gemma elaborated. "At Harvington House."

"Oh right, yeah." I nodded as if I knew the place well. "Do you reckon he'd mind if I had a go on his drums?"

"I shouldn't think so. I'm afraid it's only a starter kit and I don't think it's been tuned for ages."

I stared at the kit, trying to understand what the hell she was talking about. How could you tune drums? I sat down on the little stool and picked up some sticks.

"Can you play?" asked Gemma.

"Er ... a bit," I lied. I banged the drums and crashed the cymbals in a random frenzy, but it wasn't fooling anybody.

"I can show you a simple rhythm if you like," said Gemma. She took my place and told me to stand close behind her. I could see CJ looking a bit jealous, so I pulled a face behind her back to prove I wasn't interested, even though I could see the lace trimming of her bra under her top.

"All rock rhythms have a four–four beat," she explained. "Tap the hi-hat with your right stick, like this – one and two and three and four. Then on the one and three, put the bass drum in with your right foot. And on the two and four, hit the snare with your left stick."

She gave me a demonstration, counting out the beats in her posh accent. Her top half was bouncing up and down; it was hard to keep my eyes fixed on her hands. "There! Now your turn."

Meanwhile, Daz had sat down at the piano and had lifted the lid without asking.

"Do you read music?" asked Gemma. "We've got heaps of books – West End musicals, Beatles Greatest Hits, loads of jazz."

"Not really," admitted Daz. "I prefer to make it up as I go along." He began a demonstration of his improvisational skill, which even I could recognize as a thinly disguised version of Chopsticks.

"Have you got an amp I could plug into?" asked CJ, waving Jason's illegally borrowed guitar hopefully around the room.

"Sorry, no. My father only plays acoustic."

"Your dad plays guitar?" I said, wide-eyed. Somehow I couldn't imagine anybody's parents being able to play a musical instrument. "What? For a living?"

"Of course not!" she laughed. "He's a GP."

I'd never met anyone whose dad was a doctor, either. I was well impressed.

"Come on, play that sequence I just taught you," Gemma purred encouragingly. I took a deep breath and started counting in my head. One–two–three–four... Feet on one and three, left stick on two and, oh shit... I just could not do it. I'd never felt such a dork in my entire sixteen years on the planet. CJ and Daz collapsed on the sofa in cruel giggles. Daz was laughing so much he had to reach for his inhaler.

"It just takes practice," said Gemma kindly.

"Yeah, well, some hope of that," I replied glumly. Now I had her sympathy it seemed like a good moment to broach the subject. I reckoned that two nights a week would probably be enough to start with. Was CJ going to ask her or should I? I was about to tell her about Salamander when we heard the front door open and two loud, jolly voices calling from the hallway.

"Hello, darling! We're back!"

Gemma swore under her breath. But, before we had a chance to make a quick escape, her dad strode into the room, wearing hefty walking boots, a dark green fleece and a grey woolly hat that made him look as if he'd been on a mountain expedition rather than blackberry-picking.

Gemma introduced us, giving him the distinct impression – without actually lying – that we were sixth formers at the boys' school.

"Hi! I'm Martin," he said, shaking us warmly by the hand. We mumbled hello and looked down at the floor as if we'd just been hauled into the headmaster's office. "So, who's the musician?" he asked, gesturing towards the guitar case.

"We all are," I replied, taking a deep breath. "We're in a band. Salamander."

"You never told me that!" cried Gemma.

"We've only just started," muttered CJ, obviously embarrassed.

"Great stuff!" enthused Martin. "So, who plays what?"

"CJ's on guitar," I explained. "Daz plays keyboards and I'm the drummer."

"And who's on vocals?" The three of us looked at each other in bewilderment.

"We haven't decided yet," I said cautiously.

"Gemma can sing, can't you, darling?" said Martin. "She was Eliza Doolittle in *My Fair Lady* at school."

"Eliza who?" said Daz.

"It's a musical," explained Gemma, going slightly pink. "I wouldn't sing like that if I were in Salamander."

"I think it'd be great to have a female vocalist," I said rashly. CJ and Daz shot me an angry glare. Yes, I knew I should have waited till the band had talked it through in private, but this was our big chance. With Gemma as our singer, we'd have no problem practising in her music room. It was too good an opportunity to miss.

"Perhaps you lads better think it over before deciding," said Martin.

"It is your band, after all," beamed Gemma. "It's up to you."

There was a long expectant pause, during which Daz and CJ stared furiously at the floor.

"Why don't we discuss it over dinner!" Martin rubbed his hands eagerly. "It's only fusilli with roasted Mediterranean vegetables, but you're all welcome to stay."

CJ and Daz instantly remembered they had buses to catch.

"Perhaps we can tempt you, Liam?" he twinkled. I had only eaten a bowl of Sugar Puffs all day and was starving hungry. But I knew I couldn't cope with polite conversation around the dinner table, eating food I'd never even heard of. Besides, Gemma was CJ's girl, not mine. So I said no too.

"What did you go and do that for?" cried CJ as soon as Gemma had waved us to the end of the driveway.

"If we asked her to join the band, I bet they'd virtually let us move in," I replied.

"But I don't want her to be the singer," said CJ.

"Why not? None of us can sing, can we?" CJ and Daz shook their heads. "Then what's the problem?"

"She's too good!"

"What?"

"She'll make us look crap. She can play guitar, piano and saxophone, and she's in some stupid opera group."

"We can make sure she doesn't get too big for her

boots. Just keep saying you're 'in lurv' and you'll have her eating out of your hand. Come on, we've got to go for it. We'll never find a better place to practise."

"I dunno, it's a bit of a trek," moaned Daz. "It'll cost a fortune in bus fares." He was obviously destined to be the band's finance director.

"Once her mum and dad hear us play, they'll probably kick us out," added CJ.

"No they won't. They'll love us."

"Anyway, there are no amps at her place. How can I play guitar if I can't hear it?"

"Can't you borrow Jason's amp?" I persisted.

"Yeah, but it's really weedy."

"That'll be enough for starters. Go on," I urged. "Ring Gemma. Tell her we want her to be our singer. Say we'll practise at her place, save her the bother of going out. We'll start tomorrow evening, about seven – give her time to do her homework and all that rubbish."

Five minutes later and it was sorted. CJ didn't even have to ask about using the music room; Gemma had already had the idea herself. She was dead excited – apparently she'd always wanted to be in a band. There was just one question: did we have to be called Salamander?

4

I think we had about thirty rehearsals at Gemma's place, maybe more. I can't remember exactly. It felt as if we were virtually living there for a while, although we were never invited to stay overnight. We'd go up there after college three or four times a week, refusing Martin's offer of "supper", preferring to eat a bag of chips on the way. Soon our whole lives revolved around the band.

Gemma was still technically going out with CJ, but they only ever saw each other at band practices and CJ said that was "more than enough". I toyed with the idea of asking her out myself. She had just the kind of looks I usually went for – slim; dark, long wavy hair. And she was extremely bright – if you added all our GCSEs together we had fewer than Gemma was taking in the first place. But she seemed to think that being clever and talented entitled her to boss us all about, even though she was only fifteen and a girl. It wasn't long before she was getting on everyone's nerves.

Gemma retuned CJ's guitar for him and showed him

how to play a few basic chords. It was obvious that Daz couldn't play the piano to save his life, so she told him to bring his keyboard over and Martin fixed it for him in about five minutes – all it needed was a new fuse in the plug. Daz couldn't play the keyboard any better, although I thought he sounded OK when he used the distortion effect. Gemma wasn't very impressed with my pathetic efforts on the drums, either. After six weeks we had two songs. Well, one and a half to be precise – they had the same simple, boring rhythm, and I couldn't even do that properly. CJ made up the melodies, such as they were, and Gemma wrote most of the words, but they caused lots of arguments.

Gemma sang her soppy love lyrics like an out-of-breath angel, with an irritating tremble she called "vibrato". It didn't match the image we'd recently adopted at a secret band meeting after a particularly aggravating rehearsal. We decided that we played psychedelic indie–metal, although CJ quite rightly said we should resist any labelling. To be honest, the only label that could be reliably put on our music at that stage was "crap".

One Friday, Daz, CJ and I went to Scurvy Joe's as usual. It was a narrow room underneath an old Irish pub on the fringes of the town centre. All the local bands played there – they were only paid ten quid a night but rumour had it that talent scouts from record labels sometimes turned up, so nobody ever dared to ask for more. It was an awful venue for live music – too small with terrible acoustics – but I liked Scurvy Joe's. As soon as I walked in I felt at home. It was a bit like a youth club, only better because they'd serve just about anybody, even Daz, who was short and skinny and looked about thirteen. Charlie, a red-faced bloke with a huge beer gut, had been organizing gigs there for about twenty years. He'd been through punk, disco, hip-hop, indie–pop, grunge, metal, techno, funk, garage – you name it. He seemed to have no musical tastes of his own, not caring what was played as long as the kids kept coming in.

Over the last year or so, Scurvy Joe's had been taken over by the skater crowd – kids like myself who hung around on the library steps. We were easy to spot: longish hair, ripped, baggy jeans that were about five sizes too big, loose T-shirts, hoodies, and beanies on our heads. It was as if we were trying to hide inside our clothes. Most of us were wimps at heart, scared of the Kevs who were at that moment queuing outside Razzamataz – a tatty nightclub round the corner – trying to look hard and over eighteen. If they couldn't get in, they'd take a stroll down to Scurvy Joe's and wait for us to come out. Sometimes it got nasty. The Kevs would tax us for our bus fare or take our mobiles – those of us who hadn't had them stolen already.

Anyway, we were queuing on the staircase leading down to the gig room, waiting for the bands to finish their interminable sound checks, when I noticed this poster on the wall.

"Look!" I said. "The Battle of the Bands, November twenty-third, here. It's some kind of competition."

"'Unsigned bands only'," read CJ. "We're unsigned – we should enter!"

"Look, you only have to play three songs. We've got two already."

"What's the prize?" asked our finance director.

"Twenty hours in a recording studio."

"What's the point? It would only take about twenty minutes to record the stuff we've got," grumbled Daz.

I shook him by the shoulders. "Don't be so negative!"

I was already imagining the banks of knobs and sliders, some big-shot producer mixing together our debut CD and declaring that it was going to go down a storm. "Let's go for it! We might as well. What have we got to lose?"

The doors opened and we filed in, handing over our three quids and getting a red stamp on our right hands in return. After a few minutes, the first band started to play. They were new on the scene but already had a bit of a fan club – girls mainly, who obviously fancied the lead guitarist. They swayed along to the songs and even joined in some of the lyrics, which were full of long words and sounded like they actually meant something. We recognized some of them from the posh-school crowd at the library steps. The band's drummer, a little guy with curly blond hair and huge arm muscles, was dead impressive. Rumour had it that he was only fourteen, but I didn't want to believe it. I stood and watched him play, feeling too sick with envy to learn anything from him. I was coming to the conclusion that Daz was right, that we should forget all about entering the Battle of the Bands, when he piped up and said, "I'll do it – IF we get rid of Gemma."

"Agreed," said CJ, sipping his under-age pint of lager.

"Hang on," I interrupted. "I know she can be a bit of a pain, but you've got to admit she's good. We've got to have a singer."

"It's not singing we need, it's attitude," said Daz. "The band needs a front man – like that guy up there. He's got the crowd in the palm of his hand."

"Exactly!" said CJ. "I'll sing if you like. I couldn't be any worse."

"Yeah, but what about the drum kit?" I protested. "If we sack Gemma, we can hardly carry on practising at her house, can we? It's all right for you – you've got your gear. What am I going to play on for the next few weeks? Biscuit tins?"

"You'll have to buy a kit, Liam," announced CJ, as if it was the obvious solution.

"Oh yeah… Like how?"

"How much money you got?"

"About sixty quid in my post office account."

"That's loads of dosh," said CJ.

"But not enough for a whole drum kit. Not even second-hand."

"I know where you might get one," Daz cut in. "That creepy junk shop by the station. You know – Weird Welly's."

CJ and Daz raised a glass – decision made, problem solved. I stared into the middle distance, tapping my fingers on the table. Now I wished I'd never seen the wretched poster. What had started off as a great idea had suddenly turned into a nightmare. Our first gig was three weeks away and they wanted to dump the singer and say goodbye to half our equipment. It didn't make any sense to me, but I seemed to have been outvoted.

"OK," I sighed wearily. "I'll go down there."

5

Weird Welly was what you might call a "local character". His shop was in the oldest part of town by the
railway sidings, at the end of a row of terraced houses,
most of which were boarded up and full of rats. All the
kids knew him by sight. His face was studded with
metal, his black hair was long and straggly and his
thick, bushy eyebrows met in the middle. He was often
spotted tramping around town wearing long leather
boots, strange, flowing cloaks and heavy chains clang-
ing across his chest, which made him look like some
medieval warrior. He wasn't old, but he had a mad,
wasted look that made people want to cross the street.

A sign in the window claimed that P. R. Llewellyn
did house clearances – ANYTHING BOUGHT FOR CASH. But
Welly was also known to be heavily into black magic.
He sold mystical stuff: tarot cards, occult books, Ouija
boards, even packets of love potions and evil spells.
Rumour had it that at every full moon, Weird Welly
would take all his clothes off and run round the silver
birches in Rough Wood. There were even stories about

him dancing round certain graves in the local church-yard. Daz, whose relatives were often down the police station, said he'd been arrested for it twice.

As I stood outside Weird Welly's that Monday morning, I calculated he must have at least three drum kits in the midst of all that junk, but I still didn't fancy going in. It was as if I knew that once I stepped inside, I was going to start something I couldn't stop. It's easy to say that with hindsight, but I distinctly remember a feeling of dread, a peculiar dryness in the throat. The place was so stuffed I could hardly get in through the door. I looked around at the jumble of old wardrobes, the stained mattresses stacked up against one wall, rusty highchairs, boxes of vinyl albums and broken record players, dented saucepans, chipped crockery and useless kitchen equipment – all the things the relatives didn't want, I suppose. Nobody else seemed to want them, either. I let my eyes wander to the mystic paraphernalia on display in the corner. I could see some unusual metal objects, lots of black leather and something that looked like a crystal ball. The whole place stank of mildew mixed with strong incense. I took a deep breath and the smell invaded my lungs.

"Dragon's blood," said a voice.

I turned round to see Weird Welly lying on one of the lumpy sofas by the front door. I must have walked straight past him.

"That's the name of the smell," he added. "Ninety-nine pence for six sticks if you're interested."

Weird Welly yawned and rubbed the sleep out of his eyes. I was struck by their odd watery greenness –

they made me think of shallow rock pools. He sat up and stretched his thin, hairy arms above his head. I felt as if I'd just walked into his bedroom and woken him up.

"Got any drum kits?" I mumbled nervously.

"It's you!" he said suddenly.

"Sorry?" I looked around the shop, hoping he might be talking to somebody else, but his eyes were firmly fixed on me. Had CJ rung him and told him to expect me? What the hell did he mean? He was chuckling to himself, nodding his head, behaving as if I was some long-lost friend.

"Good to see you, Liam," he cried, throwing off an old blanket and springing to his feet. He rubbed his hands together excitedly – he was wearing tatty brown gloves with the ends chopped off the fingers. His nails were thick with dirt. God, he was giving me the creeps.

"How come you— How do you know my name?" I stuttered.

He paused and stuck out his bottom lip, as if searching for an answer. "Ah ... well ... I know your mum and dad," he replied finally.

"How come?"

"We were at school together. Well, well, well, Liam ... well, well, well..." He laughed delightedly, skipping about the room like a demented hobgoblin. "How's Sheryl?"

"Oh ... she's, er, all right, I suppose."

"Still with Garry?"

I nodded, adding the word "unfortunately" in my head.

"Is that so? And what's he doing with himself these days?" Welly continued.

"Er, nothing... He had a job but he got the sack. He's always getting the sack."

"Pity... Such a waste of talent." He blew his nose on a filthy hankie and gave me a broad, excited smile, revealing a row of rotting, yellow teeth. Then he turned the sign on the door to CLOSED and bolted the door.

"What did you do that for?" I said, looking around nervously. I was starting to wonder whether the old wardrobes and fridges were stuffed with dead, mutilated bodies. Was I going to be the next victim?

"Lots to talk about, Liam, lots to talk about," he replied. "Want a cup of tea?"

He was scaring the pants off me, but I decided it was safer to say yes. I think Welly always had some power over me, right from the beginning. Weeks later, I asked him if he just conjured up some spell to draw me to his shop. But he just smiled mysteriously and replied that he hadn't needed to. I could never get a straight answer out of Welly. He behaved as if he already knew me and had always been expecting me. But maybe I'm only saying that because of what happened later – it's hard to look back on those times now and remember how it really was.

Welly led me to his kitchen at the very back of the shop. There were about five gas cookers to choose from, but only one was connected – the oldest, dirtiest one. He put a kettle on the hob and rinsed a couple of chipped mugs under the tap.

"So, you've started a band then," he said casually.

"How do you know that?"

"You were asking about drum kits."

"Oh yes, of course."

"What does Garry think about that?"

"He doesn't know. Mum says I mustn't tell him. God knows why."

"We were in a band once. Garry, Shez and me."

I laughed in disbelief. "You've got to be kidding."

"Straight up... Garry played lead guitar, Shez was our singer and I was on keyboards. Stride was our name." Welly chuckled quietly. "What a sight we looked. We bleached streaks in our hair and Garry even wore eyeliner."

I didn't say anything for a few moments. Try as I might, I couldn't conjure up the image in my head. My mum and dad in a band together? My dad wearing make-up? It was impossible. "No, I can't believe it," I said eventually. "We are talking about the same Garry Condie?"

"That's right... I had an idea they wouldn't have mentioned it." Welly bent down to open the door of one of the fridges. There was no dead body inside, just a pint of milk and the foil tin of a half-eaten Chinese takeaway. "Milk and sugar?" I nodded and he searched around for a spoon.

"But ... but ... it doesn't make sense... When was this?"

"Mid-eighties. We were about your age. We played loads of gigs, won a local competition... Even made a demo tape. We were good. Everyone said so. We had a real future."

I looked at him in astonishment, peering closely into his eyes. Was this some kind of joke? But he looked serious enough, his gaze lost for a moment in the past.

"So what happened?"

"We split up."

"Why?"

"We lost our drummer."

"You mean he left?"

"No. He died… He was Garry's best friend, you see. We all took it hard, but Garry never got over it. Went to pieces, swore that music was the enemy – vowed he'd never pick up a guitar again." Welly handed me my mug, but the handle was hot and my hand was shaking. I immediately set it down by the sink and leant back heavily against the fridge.

We stood in silence for what felt like ages, while I listened to my heart thumping in my chest. I was in a state of shock. But suddenly I understood something that had been bugging me for weeks. Mum didn't want Dad to know about Salamander because she didn't want him upset. It would bring back bad memories, stuff he'd obviously been suppressing for years. She was protecting him as usual, protecting us from each other – although why she still bothered about that foul git I couldn't understand.

"Have you still got the demo tape?" I asked. The words came out in a squeaky tremble. I took a gulp of the hot, sweet tea and tried to clear my throat. But I only managed to burn the roof of my mouth.

"Yes. Want to hear it?"

I nodded. Welly pushed aside a tatty curtain and disappeared into another back room. I could hear him rummaging through drawers and cursing. A few minutes later he emerged triumphant and beckoned me to follow him to the front of the shop, where there was an old hi-fi unit.

"I think this works," he mumbled, untangling leads and searching for the electric socket. The plug wouldn't reach, so he had to lift it onto a wobbly dressing table.

Even though I'd never heard my mum sing, I instantly knew it was her voice. It was a typical eighties sound – very artificial and metallic. And there were sections where you could hear my dad playing some pretty mean guitar. The keyboards sounded sharp, if a little monotonous, and in the background was the pulsing rhythm of the drums, like a steady heartbeat... It was strange to think that the drummer had died shortly afterwards. In a way, everyone in the band was dead. There was nothing left of the old Sheryl and Garry. And as for Welly... God knows what had happened to him.

"What was the drummer's name?" I asked.

"We called him Murph." Welly handed me the tape. "You can have this – I've got loads. Keep meaning to throw them out, but somehow..." His voiced tailed off.

"Thanks."

"I'll keep an eye out for a drum kit. Call in again, eh? Soon."

"Yeah, I will."

I sat on the 95 bus back to college, my head spinning with questions – things I wanted to go back and ask

Welly, things I was desperate to talk to Mum about. It was all such a long time ago, but it still mattered. How could my dad have been so struck down with grief that it had made him turn against music forevermore? I was in such a state I missed my stop and had to walk all the way back up the hill.

"Well?" asked CJ, as I walked into the college coffee bar. "Did you get one?"

"One what?"

"A drum kit, you dork!"

I shook my head. "Welly's looking out for one for me."

"Don't let him get you into his clutches." Daz laughed. "He's into all sorts of dodgy stuff, you know. Black magic."

"He seemed pretty safe to me."

I wanted to tell them about Stride, but it all sounded so ridiculous, so unlikely, I didn't know where to start. "What we got this afternoon?" I asked, trying to change the subject.

"Film Studies," groaned Daz. "I'm giving it a miss."

"Me too." I finished off my Coke, squashing the can thoughtfully in my hand before hurling it in the general direction of the bin. The woman behind the counter shouted at me to pick it up, but I had more important things to worry about. "I'm going home," I said. "How about you?"

"Might as well," said CJ, getting up.

"You coming with us, Daz?" I asked.

He shook his head and a greasy strand of hair fell over his eyes. Daz spent most of his time in the coffee bar, reluctant to leave in case anything interesting happened. It never did.

It had just turned November and was getting dark earlier each day. The sky was a mixture of deep blue slashed with smoky orange – not a proper sunset, just a haze of pollution. In the distance we could hear kids letting off fireworks in the street. I felt cold and wished for the third time that day that I had a proper coat.

"If I told you my mum and dad had once been in a band, what would you think?" I said to CJ as we crossed the road by the play area.

"I'd think you were winding me up," he replied.

"That's what Weird Welly told me. He said he was in the band with them."

"Never!"

"They made a demo tape. I've got it here." I held up the tape I'd been fingering in my pocket for the last few hours, as if it were a magic charm. "It's very Eighties. Not our kind of music, but it's all right. They're more together than us."

"That's not saying much."

"Mum sang, Dad played guitar and Weird Welly was on keyboards. It's definitely her voice."

"No way!"

"They were all best friends. Can you believe that?"

"I didn't think Weird Welly had friends."

"Well, they're not friends any more. They had this drummer called Murph and he died. The band split up after that... But what I want to know is – why?"

"Because one of them was dead!"

"Yeah, but Welly's not telling me everything. I know

he's not. He behaves like he already knows me, like we're already mates."

"Perhaps you knew him when you were a kid."

"I don't think so…"

We took the short-cut alley and walked straight into an icy tunnel of wind.

"Do you think I should say anything to Mum?"

"Yeah, why not?"

"I want to talk to her about it, but something's stopping me."

"Can't see what the big deal is myself," muttered CJ. "Are you going to play us this tape or what?"

We went back to CJ's house. It was a carbon copy of mine on the outside but utterly different on the inside. CJ's parents both worked and it was obvious that they had more money than mine. CJ's dad was heavily into gadgets. He had this amazing television and DVD player – it was so big it took up half the lounge. But his pride and joy was the custom-built sound system – for CDs, minidiscs, tapes and vinyl. There were speakers in the bathroom, bedrooms and kitchen, so you could hear music all over the house. Everyone else was out, so we put on Stride's demo tape at full volume and ran round the place, listening to it in every room.

"Are you sure that's your mum singing?" called CJ from the loo. "She's got a good voice."

"This track's the best… We could almost mosh to this one!" I shouted back from his parents' bedroom.

"Not in there we couldn't," replied CJ. "Come downstairs before you break something."

"Don't Let Me Go" was the last track on the tape. It started off slowly and then sped up into a frenzy. The drumming was really impressive. I tried to beat out the rhythm on the kitchen table but it was too fast.

"Is that the drummer that died?" asked CJ.

"It must be," I said.

"What did he die of?"

"I don't know. I forgot to ask..." Suddenly a cold shiver ran across the back of my neck. "Is there a window open or something?"

"The heating's off, that's all. It's always freezing in here during the day."

I turned the tape off.

"What did you do that for?" moaned CJ. "I was getting into that track."

"Sorry," I replied. "I've got to get home. There are things I need to find out."

CJ looked me up and down. "You feeling OK?"

I shrugged. I couldn't describe how I was feeling – just strange.

I left CJ's house and went back to my place. The lights were on in the front room, so I guessed Mum had got back from work. I decided I was going to go for the shock tactics – I'd bring down my CD player and put the tape on full blast. Then she'd have to talk about Stride. Mum was in the kitchen, combing Zoe's wet hair. The room stank of chemicals and Zoe was snivelling as Mum tried her best to get rid of the tangles.

"They've got nits at the play group again," she explained. "Your tea'll be late."

"That's OK."

I was hesitating. Mum was looking even more tired and fed up than usual. I couldn't just spring it on her – it wasn't fair.

"Mum?" I ventured. "Can I play you some music?"

"Better not, love," she said quietly. "Your dad's in the lounge. He's in a terrible mood. He got chucked out the pub for arguing with the landlord."

I sighed. "What was it over this time?"

"A packet of smoky bacon crisps."

I ran upstairs and lay on my bed, feeling down and defeated. I plugged the earphones into my CD player, so that I could listen to the tape without being heard. I inserted the cassette and pressed *play*, turning the sound up as far as it would go without distorting. I let the music move into my head and gave myself over to it completely. As soon as the side ended, I flicked the tape over and carried on with no more than a few seconds' break. I must have played the tracks twenty times at least. I waved imaginary drumsticks in the air and tried my best to copy Murph's extravagant rhythms. I strummed along with Garry's guitar solos and moved my fingers up and down an invisible keyboard. By the end of the evening I knew all the words and could sing along with sixteen-year-old Sheryl, although I didn't dare raise my voice above a whisper.

Something weird was happening to me. The music was bringing tears to my eyes, but it wasn't the lyrics that were making me sad; it was the whole sorry situation. When they made that demo, they must have been so full of hope. They couldn't have thought for a moment that they'd end up in a revolting little house on a horrible estate, that Shez would be working in a clothing factory and Garry would be on the dole, drinking away his giro and getting into stupid fights. It was such a mean, useless existence that it made me want to cry. I wanted to go downstairs and give Mum an enormous hug, to tell her how much I loved her. I was even starting to feel strangely affectionate towards my dad. I wanted to play them their music and unlock their memories. I wanted to know what happened all those years before I was born. At last we'd have something in common, something to share. And who knows – maybe we would finally understand each other. But some inner authority was stopping me, telling me it was impossible. It was too risky – dangerous even. I had to keep the secret, and yet I didn't know why.

6

We had our next band practice the following evening. It was Bonfire Night and feeble fireworks were shooting into the sky from back gardens and parks all over town. Everywhere, that is, except the Drive. As we made our way up the wide, leafy, litter-free road, we realized that the place was uncannily quiet. People who lived round here didn't seem to care much for fireworks. They probably thought they were cheap and common, that they caused nasty accidents and frightened animals. Or perhaps it was just that people with decent jobs and expensive cars didn't need a box of sparklers and bangers to brighten up their lives.

Gemma's mother opened the door with a glass of white wine in her hand. She greeted us wearily and told us to park our smelly trainers in the porch. Gemma was "warming up" in the music room. She did this before every practice – singing scales like an opera singer and making funny clicking noises with her tongue "to get her articulation going", or so she claimed. I had tried to point out that the whole point of rock music was that nobody could understand the words, but it was like talking to a brick wall.

"I think we should start working on a new song," she declared as soon as we walked into the room.

"We can't play the ones we've got yet," muttered Daz.

"Too right," nodded CJ.

"I agree with Gemma," I said.

Daz and CJ glared at me, as if I was betraying ten years of friendship. I took no notice.

"And this is what I want us to play. It's called 'Don't Let Me Go'." I took out the demo tape and walked over to the sound system. "It's got exactly the right combination of instruments – guitar, keyboards, drums. It's even got female vocals."

"I thought we didn't do covers," remarked Gemma acidly. "At least, that's what you said when I wanted to do that Britney Spears song."

"This is different," I insisted. "It's good. Just shut up for once and listen, will you?" I played the track at full volume and tried not to sing along. CJ smiled knowingly at me, while Gemma looked at the floor, clearly offended. But her frown gradually melted and by the end of the song she was tapping her fingers on the arm of the chair.

"Where the hell did you find that?" laughed Daz. "Weird Welly's?"

"Yes, as it happens… What do you think?"

"It's too difficult," pronounced Gemma. "For you three, I mean – the vocal line's easy."

"I'm sure we can learn it," I insisted. "We've got

just over two weeks. I know the other two songs need finishing, but if we work hard…"

My voice tailed off. Daz and CJ were giving me meaningful stares from the sofa. I suddenly realized what I'd said.

"What do you mean, two weeks?" said Gemma.

"Oh, nothing. I meant, we should be able to nail it in two weeks."

"Or three, or four – there's no time limit. But two weeks should do it," agreed Daz, making it worse.

"What's going on?" Gemma looked from one to the other of us.

Nobody wanted to meet her gaze. There was a long pause.

"Nothing's going on. Stop being so suspicious, will you?" said CJ, standing up and putting his arm round his so-called girlfriend's shoulder. He planted a tactical kiss on her cheek. "Let's just play some music, eh?"

"So you all want to cover this song?"

"Yes," I said firmly. "We do."

"Yeah, why not?" agreed CJ. "I like it. It's good. It'll get people dancing, if, er, we ever perform it, that is…"

"But we've got to learn how to play it," said Gemma. "It's not like the music's been written down or anything."

"That wouldn't make any difference," said Daz. "None of us can read music."

"I can," Gemma pointed out.

"I know it's complicated," I admitted, "but do you think you could work it out for us, Gem?" I gave her one of my special appealing looks, usually reserved for extracting forgiveness from Mum.

"Probably." Gemma flicked her long, dark hair behind her back. Her anger and suspicion had vanished – not only had I acknowledged her superior musical ability, I had set her a challenge. "We'll start with the keyboards first."

We listened to the track again and again, while Gemma sat and experimented on the piano. It wasn't long before she'd worked out the melody and most of Daz's chords. Whether he could play them was another matter. Then she went to work on the guitar section. CJ couldn't really be bothered to learn his bits properly and quickly became impatient. I realized that Garry had been a pretty decent guitarist in his time. As for my drumming solo, well, it was virtually impossible to get anywhere near Murph's level of skill.

"He's sticking in loads of paradiddles," she exclaimed. "You'll have to cut the solo and go for the basic rhythm, Liam, or we'll never get anywhere."

By the end of the evening, we were playing a sort of simplified, kiddies' version of "Don't Let Me Go". It didn't sound much like the original, but that was a good thing in a way. The song had lost its shiny metallic edge and was almost grungy. I liked it. We all liked it. Now we had our third song for the Battle of the Bands – at least we would have with a couple of weeks' prac- tice. But we'd never have managed it without Gemma. I was starting to feel bad about ditching her; it didn't seem right.

"We could dump her straight after the Battle of the Bands," I offered as we sat on the bus on the way home. "None of us has practised singing, and we need a girl's voice for 'Don't Let Me Go'. It's going to be our best song."

"That's because we didn't write it," replied Daz, munching his way through a chicken kebab. "Who did, by the way?"

"I'm not sure exactly. Probably my mum and dad."

Daz nearly choked on a piece of shredded cabbage. I thumped him several times on the back and told him the whole story.

"No way! No way!" he spluttered, in between coughs.

"She really helped us tonight," I said cautiously. "Gemma, I mean. She's the only one of us with any real musical talent. I'm not sure we can afford to do without her."

"Either she goes or I do," announced Daz. He couldn't compete with Gemma on musical terms, but the three of us had been mates since infant school. He knew there was no way we'd back Gemma against him.

"OK," I sighed. "But not just yet. I'm going to see Welly tomorrow. Maybe he'll have found me a kit."

Welly hadn't found me a kit. I don't think he'd even been looking for one. Old folks didn't usually leave drum kits, just smelly mattresses and wonky wardrobes. Anyway, selling me something was the last thing on his mind.

"Come in, Liam, shut the door. Turn the sign round," he said as soon as I arrived. "How's things?"

"OK... Nothing much has happened. I've been playing the tape a lot."

"Like it?"

"Yeah. 'Don't Let Me Go' is my favourite."

"Mine too. Could have been number one... Too late now, of course."

"Well, you never know." I grinned. "We're doing a new version of it. For the Battle of the Bands."

Welly breathed in sharply. "When's that happening?" he muttered, looking away.

"November the twenty-third at Scurvy Joe's. Will you come?"

"Oh yes, I'll be there."

Welly seemed rattled, as if I'd said something I shouldn't have or broken some taboo.

"What's wrong?"

"Nothing, nothing. Want a beer? I bought a couple of bottles. I was expecting you to come back." He rushed off in search of a bottle opener. I sat on a lumpy sofa and took off my beanie.

"Have you got any skateboards?" I shouted. "Only mine got busted and I can't afford a new one."

"Skateboards... No, don't think so... You don't need a glass, do you?" He came back into the shop and sat beside me. "Cheers!"

"How did Murph die?" I asked after a pause.

Welly swallowed hard.

"Car accident."

"Were you there? Did you see it?"

"Yeah... We all did. It gave me nightmares for months. I don't like remembering it even now."

"Sorry, I didn't mean to—"

"No, no, you're entitled to ask... Poor kid was dead

by the time the ambulance arrived. Never had a chance. He's buried up at the Catholic church. St Cedd's."

"I know it – that's near where my nan lives."

"It's near where we all lived, once upon a time… We were good mates. You know, in and out of each other's houses, walking to school together every morning…" Welly sighed fondly and let out a large burp. "Want to go and see his grave?"

"Well … I don't know." I hesitated. I didn't care much for graveyards – they gave me the creeps.

"Come on," said Welly, "I'll give you a lift."

St Cedd's was on the top of a hill – an ugly church with a windswept, overgrown graveyard overlooking the industrial estate. I remember my primary school teacher Mrs Featherstone telling us that churches were always built on the highest land in the village so that the worshippers could be as close as possible to God. In those days, they must have imagined that He lived in the skies – a kind, old gentleman with a long, white beard, floating around on a cloud. Did they really believe that God was looking down on them, smiling approvingly as the sound of their hymns drifted upwards on the breeze? If He was up there now, He was probably tutting and shaking His head. There was graffiti on the noticeboard, beer cans and chip wrappers littered the graveyard, and the church door had been padlocked to keep out tramps. It looked abandoned, but Welly assured me that they still held mass twice a week.

I'd passed St Cedd's hundreds of times but had never been inside – probably because it was Catholic.

Not that my family ever visited a church of any denomination. I wasn't even christened, although Mum always put me down as "Church of England" on official forms. There was a time when I believed in God, when I was about five and had just started at primary school. I learnt all the hymns with jolly calypso beats and thanked God several times a week for making us all so "special" – religion seemed easy then. At secondary school we plodded through world faiths until they became a confused blur – I could never remember which lot grew their hair and wore little daggers, who fasted, and who didn't eat pork or drink alcohol. Words like "nirvana" or "karma" made me think of rock bands more than spiritual salvation. When it came to Christianity, I had no trouble believing that Jesus had existed – a healer, a wise man, a revolutionary, even. But all that rising from the dead and ascending into heaven to sit at God's right hand – I was sure it was all crap.

Welly stopped the car but left the engine running. He didn't seem in any hurry to get out. I sensed that he'd been about to tell me something important but had decided against it. We sat in silence while I stared at the grubby, ill-kept tombstones. Hundreds of dead people, most of them long since forgotten. When I was a kid I couldn't imagine dying. My friends had had a few brushes with mortality – Daz once had some hamsters that ate each other, and CJ's goldfish committed suicide by jumping out of its bowl. As for humans, well, my grandparents were only in their fifties and seemed likely to last forever. There were a few kids of my age who took overdoses or hanged themselves in their bedrooms, but they were just photos in newspapers. Strangely enough, I'd been on earth for sixteen years, and I didn't actually know anyone who had died.

"Murph's grave is in the far corner," Welly said eventually. "You can't miss it. It's the only one with fresh flowers round it."

"Is this where you come to do your black magic stuff?" I asked.

"It's not black magic," he answered sharply. "It's white magic, good magic. How come you know about that?"

"Everyone knows. You're famous."

"Infamous, you mean."

"Is it true about you stripping off in the woods and dancing round bonfires?"

He chuckled and rolled a cigarette. "I only tried it once. Some bloke walking his dog caught me at it and called the police. They gave me a caution. But it wasn't the law that made me stop; it was the cold."

"So what do you do? Do you try to raise the dead?"

"No ... I just want a chat."

I couldn't help but smile. "Do you chat with Murph, then?"

"I try to, but he won't talk to me. He's still angry." He lit the fag with the car's cigarette lighter and put his scuffed leather boots up on the dashboard. "Others talk to me, but I'm not interested. I didn't know them when they were alive, and I don't want to know them when they're dead, either."

"Who are they?"

"Old people mainly. Sometimes it's because I've cleared out their houses. They follow their furniture to the shop, like they can't bear to be apart from their favourite armchair. They sit there mumbling at me for hours on end, some of them."

"You're winding me up."

"No, I'm not. It used to scare me. Now it just gets on my nerves."

"Do you see them?"

"Not usually. Just hear them. I've even made recordings, but when you play it back it sounds like static."

"You really are weird, aren't you?"

"So they say…"

There was a long pause.

"Aren't you going to come with me?" I asked. The car was stuffy and smoky – the heater was on full blast and it was giving me a headache.

"No, better not. Murph's mum usually turns up about now. She won't like it if she sees me. You mustn't tell her it was me that brought you here. Don't even mention my name."

"But how do you know I'm going to meet her?"

"I just do, that's all." His pale green eyes shimmered. For a moment I thought he was going to cry. "Wheels are turning, Liam," he said. "I can feel it. Now out you get."

I stood on the pavement and watched Weird Welly's car until it disappeared round a bend at the bottom of the hill. Then I walked down the litter-strewn path and onto the grass. Most of the gravestones were old and crumbling; some leant dangerously to one side. There were no large tombs, like you see in some cemeteries. The people that lived round here had never been rich. Welly was right – it was easy to spot Murph's grave. In the centre was an earthenware pot overflowing with yellow, velvety flowers. In front of the headstone itself was a vase of fresh roses and carnations, and some others that I recognized but couldn't put names to. The stone was white marble, so clean it looked like you could eat your dinner off it. I read the inscription.

In fondest memory of
Liam Murphy
Who left us 19 July 1986
Aged seventeen years.
Now we have our own angel in heaven.

7

Liam. His name was Liam. Welly had only referred to Murph by his nickname. Was that because he had forgotten his real name or because he didn't want to tell me I had been named after a dead boy? I calculated that I had been born five months after Murph's death, when Mum and Dad must have been still grieving for their friend. So why had they never mentioned my namesake to me? Why had I not been told any fond stories about their best mate Murph who had been cruelly taken from this world before his time? I stood there, mesmerized by the sight of my own name carved in the marble. It was like looking at my own grave.

"Hello?" said a quiet voice.

I started suddenly and gasped. A woman was standing behind me, about sixty years old, wearing a green scarf over her head and a beige raincoat. She was carrying a plastic bag full of flowers and a small, old-fashioned, brown handbag. She had to be Murph's mum, making her daily visit to the grave, just as Weird Welly had predicted.

"Hello," I replied gently. "You don't mind, do you?"

She shook her head slowly, staring at me with weary grey eyes, as if I was familiar to her in some way but she couldn't put her finger on it.

"Who are you?" she asked.

"Liam Condie. I'm Sheryl and Garry's son. Do you remember them? They were friends of your son. This is your son, isn't it?" I added, gesturing at the headstone.

She nodded. "Yes ... and of course I remember... They named you after him."

We stared at the headstone together in silence for a few moments.

"Are they married now?"

"Oh, yeah. Have been for ages."

"And are they well?"

"Yes, sort of. Mum works at Bradshaw's; Dad hasn't got a job at the moment."

"That's a shame... I haven't seen either of them in years. Your father was forever round our house when he was a lad. I think I fed him more often than his own mother... Yes, he was a nice boy, Garry, a nice boy..." Her voice drifted off towards the past.

As Mrs Murphy knelt down I heard both her knees crack. She put the vase to one side and picked out a few of the flowers whose petals had fallen off or were yellowing at the edges. She replaced them with pink roses, which looked rather girlish and not quite in keeping with a rock drummer's image. Then Mrs Murphy took some cleaning materials out of her handbag. She squirted liquid cleaner over the headstone, wiping it with soft, loving sweeps before using a toothbrush to dig into the crevices of the inscription. Finally she took out a dry cloth and polished the marble until it shone and smelt strangely of lemons.

"So what brought you up here, then?" she asked.

"I just wanted to see the grave."

"Pay your respects?"

"Yes ... I suppose so."

"That's not a common thing these days ... respect. I'm the only one who comes here now. For the first couple of years some of his friends came, but they soon grew up and forgot. But you never forget losing a child. Never."

"It must have been hard," I mumbled back uselessly.

"It's not natural. It's not the way things should be. He should be tending my grave, not me his... But this was how the Lord wanted it... She sighed deeply. "It's a pity that they keep the church locked. We could have lit a candle for him together."

I watched her as she carefully tidied everything away. Every fallen petal was put into the carrier bag, every stray leaf and lump of moss. I imagined her bringing the vacuum cleaner here and hoovering around the headstones as if they were furniture. She stood up and rubbed the small of her back absent-mindedly.

"Mrs Murphy?" I ventured. "Do you remember anything about the band – Stride?"

"Of course I do. They always practised in our house. Deafening it was, too, at times. Not that I minded. I loved to hear them."

"And did my dad really play guitar?"

"Yes. And your mother sang. She had a lovely voice. I still play their tape, you know. On special days. And then, of course, there's the scrapbook."

"What's that?"

"Oh, clippings from the newspapers, posters, a few photographs... Liam liked to collect things, liked to set everything down. Sometimes I wonder if he knew he wasn't long for this life..."

"I'd love to look at it," I said quietly, not daring to meet her eyes.

"Would you now?" said Mrs Murphy, looking at me closely as if trying to make up her mind. "Then why don't you come back with me, Liam? It's only a few streets away."

Her name was Mary, although I only ever called her Mrs Murphy. As we walked along she told me that she was a widow and had been so for many years. Her husband had died from a heart attack when they were visiting relatives in Ireland and was buried over there. Liam had been their only son. It was a cruel lot that had been measured out to Mary Murphy. I think she would have killed herself if somebody else had promised to take care of the grave.

Mrs Murphy lived in a small terraced house on the end of a long row. It was almost identical to my nan and grandad's place, so I had a pretty good idea how it would look inside. Sure enough, the front door opened straight onto a tiny lounge. Mrs Murphy told me to take a seat while she put the kettle on.

"Will you have a cup of tea?" she asked from the kitchen.

"No thanks."

"I've orange squash if you prefer."

"No, I'm all right, really. Thanks."

The room was plainly furnished – a brown velvet sofa and matching chair, a moss-green carpet, cream painted wallpaper and beige curtains. Mrs Murphy was not a woman who liked patterns or decoration. The only ornaments were some religious statues on the sideboard, jockeying for position with a faded picture of the Pope, which looked as if it had been cut out of a magazine many years ago. There were no paintings on the wall, just a large wooden crucifix and an oval gilt mirror, which hung above the gas fire.

There were a number of silver-framed photographs of her family on the shelves above the television. There was the wedding photo, of course – a young woman with dark curly hair, clinging onto her new husband's arm as they stood outside the church in what looked like a howling gale. Then there was Murph: as a baby wearing a long white gown, as a toddler playing on the sand, then as a young boy in a football shirt, riding his bike in the garden. The picture that really caught my eye was of Murph as a young teenager. He was tall and gangly, his hair down to the tip of his collar, slicked back behind his ears. He was wearing tight black trousers and a baggy white shirt with a loose tie, as if he was on his way to some family occasion and had been told to dress up. In every shot, Murph looked happy and contented – but then how else did I expect him to look? Nobody had told him he was going to die when he was seventeen.

Mrs Murphy walked back into the room carrying a tray of tea things and a large scrapbook under her arm. "There are plenty more photos in here," she said.

I suppose I was more interested in finding pictures of

my mum and dad – and of Welly, of course. But I let Mrs Murphy take me slowly through every page of Stride memorabilia.

"Now, that's a ticket for the school disco – one of their first paid gigs," she explained proudly, pronouncing "gigs" as if it were the correct technical term rather than slang. She pointed to a creased scrap of paper, torn from a brown envelope. "This shows the running order of their set when they performed at the British Legion club down the road... It's been pulled down now..."

I nodded and mmm-ed politely, my fingers itching to turn the pages, but she kept the book firmly on her lap.

"There's the leaflet for the Valentine's Evening, the first time that Stride headlined... Oh, and there's an article in the local paper... Read it... They said the band had a great future." At that point, Mrs Murphy reached for the white cotton handkerchief that was permanently tucked up her sleeve. "Here, you look at it," she sniffed, passing me the scrapbook. "Sorry, you'll have to excuse me..." She left the room.

I flicked through the pages and finally found what I was looking for – a photo of the band in action. There was my mum at the microphone, wearing a ton of make-up on her face, her hair short and spiky with blonde streaks across the front. Dad was bending forwards, one skinny leg in front of the other, his eyes fixed on the neck of the guitar, his hair flopping forwards, obscuring his face. It was a pity – I had been desperate to see him wearing eyeliner. And sitting at the back behind a massive drum kit was Murph. His face looked red with effort, his mouth gulping open for air, his arms blurred in movement. The sticks were raised as if he was about to crash the cymbal. Welly was not in the picture, but on the edge of the photo I could see a dark rectangular object which could have been the end of a keyboard on a stand. I imagined him, standing to one side, pounding the keyboards, smiling confidently at the crowd. I wondered who had taken the photograph. Welly? Mrs Murphy herself? It seemed unlikely. This was a proper gig in a paying venue, somewhere dark and crowded. The photographer had needed to use the flash – everyone in the picture had red dots in their eyes.

Mrs Murphy returned and stood looking over my shoulder.

"Where was this taken?" I asked.

"I've no idea, Liam. Somewhere in town, I suppose."

"It must have been noisy, practising in this house. Didn't your neighbours complain?"

"Not really. Old Mrs Winters on that side was deaf; she's passed on now, God rest her soul. I made them play with the windows shut, mind you. Even in the summer." She paused and stared at the net curtains. In her mind, she could hear the music playing – the drum beat thumping through the floorboards, the strains of keyboard melody floating down the stairs. Her eyes were filling with tears again. I closed the scrapbook and stood up.

"Thanks, but I think I should go now."

"Do you want to see his room?" she said quietly.

Mrs Murphy led me up the narrow staircase as if we were making a solemn pilgrimage to a holy place. "I haven't touched a thing – only to dust, of course. I keep it spotless, cleaner than it used to be and that's the truth. But otherwise, it's just as he left it." She took a deep breath, preparing herself to face the certain surge of emotion, and opened the door. I felt as if I was stepping into a large tomb. The room was dark and gloomy, the curtains drawn across the windows although it was the middle of the day.

"It was early evening when he last left the room," she said. "He said he didn't know when he'd be back."

"I suppose none of us know," I replied thoughtfully.

The room smelt strongly of the same cleaning fluid that Mrs Murphy had used to wipe the headstone – death with a twist of lemon. She drew back the curtains and a burst of winter sunshine illuminated the furniture. There were band posters all over the walls, a brightly striped duvet cover on the bed, two large beanbags on the carpet, a white wardrobe plastered with stickers...

But there was something far more remarkable sitting in the room – I couldn't take my eyes off it. It was a drum kit – deep red and silver, with the word "Stride" painted in black across the front of the bass drum. The pieces shone like new, as if they had only just been taken out of their boxes. And a pair of drumsticks lay temptingly on the bass tom – placed there by Murph himself, no doubt. I was stunned. This was exactly what I had been searching for. Had Weird Welly known that Mrs Murphy had kept the drums all this time? Had he led me to the grave, knowing I would meet her? Either way, I immediately felt that the drums belonged to me. I had been meant to find them. Suddenly, I wanted this drum kit more than I had ever wanted anything in my entire life.

I took a few deep breaths. Mrs Murphy was watching me, waiting for my reaction. We were both trembling, but it was hardly surprising – the bedroom was freezing cold. Mary may have left everything just as it was when Murph died, but at least she hadn't been crazy enough to heat an empty room. Not that it felt empty. It was thick with atmosphere, so strong that you could almost touch it – seventeen years of memories tightly packed into a small square space, leaving scarcely enough air for the living to breathe.

"It's a beautiful kit," I whispered. "Must have cost a fortune."

"It was the best I could afford at the time – for his seventeenth birthday. He only played it for a few months. I was still paying off the loan two years after he passed away."

"Would you mind if I had a go?"

Mrs Murphy pursed her lips.

"Oh, well, I don't know... I'm not sure..."

"Please? I'd like to hear the sound in this room. I want to imagine what it was like."

"Nobody has touched them, you see, nobody. Not since the day—"

"Just a short go? Please?"

Mrs Murphy summoned up what little courage she had left. "All right then ... seeing as how you're Garry's boy and all."

"Thanks." I edged my way around the kit and sat on the stool. Murph must have been taller than I was because it was too low. I wanted to adjust the height, but it seemed like sacrilege. Mary backed away towards the door, keeping her eyes on me the whole time. I picked up the sticks and went over my only rhythm sequence in my head, the one I played for "Don't Let Me Go". It was going to sound pathetic but it would have to do.

I began to play.

How can I explain what happened next? It wasn't magic. It wasn't a hallucination. I didn't see anything or hear anyone speak or feel anyone else's hands on the sticks. All I know is, it wasn't me that played those drums on that November afternoon. It was Murph. There was simply no other explanation. I couldn't play like that – I didn't know how. The rhythms were fast and precise, the rolls spectacular. The sound filled the entire room with an extraordinary energy. I played drags and strokes, ruffs, paradiddles and flamacues – all the stuff Gemma had tried to teach me without success. My wrists felt as if they were on fire, my fingers swelled, both arms ached from shoulder to fingertips.

I was possessed by the spirit of Liam Murphy. He'd been waiting in his bedroom for all those years for someone to come and sit at the drum kit and pick up his sticks. It didn't frighten me; it didn't make me leap up from the stool and run out of the house screaming. Besides, I don't think I could have moved if I had tried. Murph had me cemented to the stool, and he wasn't going to release me until he had played enough. It was exhilarating, inspiring. At last I could play!

When it was over and Murph let me put down the sticks, I sat at the kit, trembling, in a stupefied daze. Mrs Murphy was staring at me, tears rolling relentlessly down her dry, wrinkled cheeks.

"You play well," she said finally. "Almost as good as my son."

I went straight to Welly's place and found him unloading yet another pile of crappy furniture from his battered old van. He took the news very calmly, nodding his head as I told him my strange tale.

"I don't know why it didn't occur to me before," he said, dragging a huge wooden wardrobe across the pavement. "Of course Murph would use his drumming to get in touch... Eh, give us a hand with this, will you?" I took the other end and we carried it into the shop.

"Did you know his mum had kept his drum kit?"

"No, of course I didn't... Over there, in the corner, please... I remember it, though. He loved that kit – it meant the world to him. I can imagine why his spirit didn't want to let it go. Just like my old people and their favourite armchairs." Welly was panting, out of breath. He sat down on a pile of plastic garden seats and rolled a cigarette.

"So you don't think I'm making it up?" I pressed.

"Why should I?"

"I couldn't have imagined it?"

"You could, but I don't think you did. In fact, I'm sure you didn't..."

"I've no idea how long it went on for, that's the odd thing. It may only have been for a few seconds, or it may have gone on for hours."

"It's irrelevant," said Welly. "You were in a place where time doesn't exist."

"You mean, some kind of magic was at work?"

"This has nothing to do with magic, Liam. It's all about Time..." He lit the rollie and took a long, considered drag. "You see, I discovered many years ago that there are no such things as Past, Present and Future. They're meaningless concepts in the wider scheme of things. Will tomorrow happen because of yesterday, or did yesterday happen because of tomorrow? It's impossible to say. Nobody believes that Time is a long straight line with a beginning, middle and end. That idea went out of the window long ago."

"Did it?" I was confused. Welly gave out a dry, rasping laugh.

"You've probably heard that time travel is theoretically possible – mathematically calculable. As yet, nobody's invented a machine that can transport our bodies back and forth in time – I doubt that they ever will. But, spiritually, it's happening all the time. That's what you experienced today. I don't know whether you wandered into the past, or Murph slipped into the future – in a way it doesn't matter. All I know is that if there are no beginnings then there can be no endings. Our bodies may die and decay, but our spirits live on. They can travel where they wish, backwards and forwards, probably even to other universes. In that sense we are all immortal. So, you mustn't be afraid, Liam. Please, whatever happens to you, try not to be afraid."

"How can I be afraid?" I replied. "I don't understand a word you're saying."

"Nor do I, most of the time," said Welly, rising and walking back to his van. He shut the doors and fastened them with a large padlock. "Moments of enlightenment, that's all I ever have. Brief flashes of understanding in a world of confusion and darkness." Welly pointed up at the grey November skies and traced the thin curve of sunlight that was illuminating the edge of a rain cloud. "But they're worth waiting for, Liam, I promise you that."

"What is this all about?" I asked. "You know something, don't you? You're not telling me the whole story."

"That's because I don't know the whole story," he replied. "Not yet. But the wheels are turning, that much I do know. The wheels are turning…"

I left him and walked home, but when I reached my front door I couldn't remember how I'd got there. My brain was doing cartwheels in my head, spinning round and round to a tight four–four beat. I was incredibly excited and yet deeply troubled. Welly might have been an old hand at communicating with spooks and spirits, but this was new territory for me. It was taking me well beyond my comfort zone, and I wasn't sure I could handle it. Part of me wanted to forget Murph, give up the band, settle down at college and never see Welly again. But I couldn't. Murph's spirit had contacted me that afternoon and he wanted me to go back and play those drums again.

8

The two weeks leading up to the Battle of the Bands were very strange.

I was like a spy, a double agent moving between enemies – telling lies, keeping secrets and spinning webs of deceit. For a start, Mrs Murphy had no idea that I was friendly with Welly. When I casually let his name slip during one of our Stride chats, she told me that he had "sold his soul to the Devil" as if it was a matter of indisputable fact. "If he ever approaches you, Liam, you must call the police," she insisted. Yet when I wasn't drinking tea and nibbling custard creams at Mrs Murphy's, I was at Welly's shop, burning incense and discussing concepts of time travel through the spirit world.

I was too embarrassed to tell CJ and Daz about my weird experience in Murph's bedroom. CJ would have laughed at me and Daz would have claimed that I was under Welly's evil spell. So I made excuses not to meet them at the library steps, saying that while I didn't have a skateboard there was no point. None of us went to college very often – I just couldn't get interested in my courses. Sooner or later we were going to be chucked out, but I didn't care. None of it seemed relevant any more. I was still committed to the band practices, but now they were based on deceit, too. I felt awkward about going to Gemma's house. She kept talking about putting a set together and where we might give our debut performance. We nodded and listened, all the time knowing that we'd signed up for the Battle of the Bands and were going to dump her the following week.

As for Mum and Dad, well, they didn't know about any of it – but that was nothing new. My feelings towards them had changed, although they didn't appear to have noticed. I didn't feel angry with them any more – I pitied them. Whenever I looked at them now, I saw them as teenagers with blond streaks in their hair and black liner round their eyes. When Garry lost his temper with me over something, I just pictured him wearing make-up and a silver bomber jacket, and all the anger would float out of me. A couple of times I was on the brink of telling him that I knew about Stride, but I preferred to keep the secret – it gave me a kind of power.

I spent several afternoons with Mrs Murphy, poring over countless family photo albums and the beloved scrapbook, making polite comments and listening to stories about her childhood in Ireland, all the time desperately wanting to have another go on the drum kit. She never offered, and I couldn't bring myself to ask. I felt as if the tomb upstairs had been resealed and would not be opened to public view for many years to come. I liked Mrs Murphy; I could tell she was a kind soul, but she was also a grief addict. Her trips to the church-yard were a daily fix that she couldn't do without. She went to Mass as often as she could and constantly begged the Virgin Mary to care for her son in heaven. I couldn't imagine what sins she confessed to the priest – probably that she hadn't cried enough or had caught herself laughing at one of my jokes. I think she looked forward to my visits because they provided fuel for her obsession. I was fast becoming part of her grieving ritual. Tea and tears, that's what our afternoons together were made of. No matter how I tried to steer the conversation away from Murph, she would find a way to drag us back. She wanted to wallow in her pool of sadness. I could tell that it wasn't healthy; I knew I should leave her be. But I couldn't stay away.

It was the day before the big gig. The morning was cold and wintry, the skies heavy with greyness, and it was about to bucket down with rain. I bought a small bunch of flowers from the petrol station and caught the bus up to Corsfield. I had an odd, sick feeling in my stomach, made worse as we swung round the corners and screeched to a halt at every stop. The windows were so covered in grime it was hard to see where we were. I felt like a blind man, trying to map the route in my head, counting off the stops. In the end I got off too early and had to trudge the rest of the way up the hill to the church. As I had hoped, the cemetery was deserted – Mrs Murphy didn't usually turn up until midday. I wanted to be on my own at the graveside, to see if Murph's spirit would make contact with me. I stuffed the flowers into the vase and studied the inscription, reading it silently again and again, as if it were a spell to raise the dead. I don't know what I was expecting – a shadowy figure rising from behind the headstone? A voice whispering at my side and a gentle tugging of my sleeve?

I stood there for several minutes, but nothing happened. It began to rain. If Murph's troubled spirit was wandering through the ether, it certainly didn't hang around here – not on a wet Thursday morning anyway. I couldn't blame him. This dull, grey place had nothing to do with his life. No, if Murph was anywhere he was in his bedroom, sitting at his drum kit, waiting for my return.

"I wasn't expecting you until this afternoon," said Mrs Murphy as she opened the door. "I'm still doing my ironing."

"I've just been to visit the grave," I explained.

"Oh, you are a good lad," she said, immediately won over. "Come in, come in."

I followed her through the back and into the kitchen. There was a small, neat pile of ironing on the dining table – sheets, a pillowcase, two plain pink blouses. I wondered if she still washed Murph's bedding but decided not to ask.

"Would you believe it," she sighed, staring into the fridge. "I've run out of milk." She paused and looked up at me expectantly, waiting for me to offer to go to the corner shop, just as any nice, obedient young man would. But I pretended not to catch the hint.

"We've got our first gig tomorrow," I said casually. "I wish you could come."

"Oh, you don't want a fuddy-duddy like me hanging around," she said. "I never went to Stride's gigs. Liam always said I'd put him off – make him nervous. I understood, but I would have liked to have heard them play properly – just once." Her eyes began to well with predictable tears. "It wasn't the same listening to them upstairs."

Upstairs. That's where I wanted to be – upstairs with Murph, playing the drums.

"Well, I can't drink tea without milk," she stated, unbuttoning her blue nylon housecoat. "I'll just pop round to the paper shop."

"OK," I replied lightly. "I'll wait here."

"Yes, yes... Just make yourself comfy." Mrs Murphy buttoned up her beige raincoat and put her purse in her pocket. "I won't be long." She hurried out of the front door, looking slightly mystified. I felt bad about not offering to go, but it was only one in a long line of deceptions. This was my only chance and I had to take it.

I only had a few minutes. The drumming would be noisy, more than likely she would hear it from across the street, so I knew I would have to stop well before she returned. I ran up the stairs and flung open Murph's door without a scrap of reverence. A blast of cold air almost knocked me back. I hesitated at the threshold. Suddenly I felt afraid. What, or who, was I going to find? But there was no time to waste. If I was going to do this thing, I had to do it now. I walked over to the drum kit and sat on the stool, half expecting it to feel warm beneath me. The sticks were sitting on the tom, just where I had left them. I picked them up and raised them in the air. "I'm ready, Murph," I whispered.

There was silence... My arms began to wilt and sunk to my sides. Where had he gone? Why wasn't he possessing me, like he did before?

"Come on, I'm ready, Murph," I repeated. "Please... We don't have long." I lifted my arms again and held my breath. I waited for the sticks to quiver in my hands, willing the surge of energy to flow from my shoulders down to the tips of my fingers. The room suddenly felt colder than ever. A deep, freezing chill engulfed me, as if somebody had just opened a door. I sensed that Murph was in the room. I felt him standing right behind me, but I was too terrified to turn round. I didn't want to see him, couldn't bear to see him...

Then a clear, calm voice in my head said, "Let's play." I tried to relax, to let Murph take control. My arms were feeling heavy as a dull pain began in my wrists and made its way towards my elbows. My hands were tingling, as if I had pins and needles. Who was holding the sticks now – him or me?

"What do you think you're doing, Liam?" said a voice.

The sticks suddenly fell onto the cymbals with an angry crash. I looked up to see Mary Murphy, still wearing her raincoat, a carton of milk trembling in her hands.

"I didn't give you permission to go tramping all over my son's things, did I?"

"No, I'm sorry," I mumbled. "I'm really sorry."

"You wait until my back is turned and you rush up here, meddling and interfering. This is my son's room. These are his private possessions!"

"Yes, I know... I'm sorry." My arms were aching badly – they felt as heavy as lead. I was sure that Murph's spirit was inside me and that he was angry with his mother for disturbing us. Or maybe he was angry with me for tricking her. Whatever the reason, there was a horrible atmosphere in the room – I had to get out.

"I didn't mean to offend you – I just wanted to play..." I muttered, squeezing past the kit and making for the door.

"You'd better not come again," Mrs Murphy said sharply. "Go home and forget him, like your father and mother did!" she shouted as I ran, stumbling down the narrow stairs. "I'm the only one that really loved him," she sobbed. "I'm the only one left who cares!"

I ran all the way to Weird Welly's: down the big hill, along the length of the High Street, dodging past shoppers and running in between the cars until I came to the railway sidings. I leant against the metal railings and tried to catch my breath. I was cold and yet sweating, my legs were hurting and my stomach ached with a stitch. I was terrified but exhilarated at the same time. The ghost of Murph was definitely in that room. I hadn't imagined it – I had really felt it.

When I got to the shop, Welly was in the middle of serving some customers. They were a young couple, not much older than me, and were looking for a load of stuff to furnish their council flat. Welly gestured at me to go out the back and wait for him. But I was hopping with impatience – if I didn't speak to him soon I was going to explode.

"It happened again!" I shouted as soon he joined me. "I sat at the drum kit and picked up the sticks. Nothing happened at first, but then gradually I felt this strange sensation in my arms, like liquid was being poured into my veins. They're still aching, even now – honest!"

"OK, OK, I believe you," Welly replied. "Calm down, will you? Tell me what happened next."

"Murph's spirit took hold of the sticks, I swear. And he was just about to play when his mum walked into the room and caught me."

"You were up there without her knowing?"

"Yeah, I know I shouldn't have, but there was no other way. And he wanted me to come. He was waiting for me, Welly... I know he was waiting for me."

"I take it Mary wasn't too pleased."

"No... She told me not to come again. Now I've blown it."

"You kept his sticks, though," said Welly, gesturing at my trousers. I looked down. To my astonishment, Murph's drumsticks were poking out of the pocket of my baggy jeans.

"But ... but ... I didn't put them there..." I stuttered. "I'm sure I didn't!"

"I wouldn't worry. It looks like Murph wants you to have them," replied Welly matter-of-factly. "Fancy a beer?"

I stayed at Welly's shop all afternoon. I held the drumsticks constantly, turning them over between my fingers, hoping they would spring into action of their own accord. I even tried to bash out rhythms on the top of the old cookers and fridges, but if Murph's spirit was in the vicinity he didn't want to play.

"We're not friends any more, Murph and I. Remember?" said Welly. "He probably doesn't want to communicate with you in front of me. I doubt that he likes you being here at all."

"I'd better get going anyway," I said. "It's our last practice tonight before the gig. I'm dreading it – we're giving Gemma the elbow."

"Why get rid of her now? Don't you need her for tomorrow?" asked Welly.

"Not according to CJ and Daz, we don't. CJ reckons he can sing and play guitar at the same time. I don't think he's tried it yet. God, it could be a complete shambles."

"Best of luck, mate," said Welly. He suddenly flung his arms round me in a bear hug. He smelt of tobacco, incense and not enough baths. It was the kind of embrace you give someone that you're never going to see again. As he pulled away from me, I saw him smudge away a tear from his eye.

"Whatever happens," he said, "you mustn't be afraid. Come and find me. I'll be there."

"I'm not nervous. I'm looking forward to it," I replied lightly. "We'll have a drink in the bar afterwards. You can give me your verdict on our version of 'Don't Let Me Go'."

He nodded and forced a yellow smile.

And that was the last conversation I ever had with Weird Welly – depending on your concept of Time, of course.

When the three of us arrived at Gemma's house that evening, she was already waiting for us in the music room.

"So you decided to turn up," her mum commented sarcastically as we kicked off our trainers and padded across the hall.

"She's found out," I whispered to CJ. But there was no time to talk tactics – we'd been ambushed. Gemma was sitting at the piano, fiddling nervously with the keys. As we entered the room she gave us a tragic heroine look – conveying deep hurt and great personal courage in a single tremble of her bottom lip.

Martin was leaning on the wide bay windowsill, still wearing his work clothes – a brown suit, white shirt and over-jolly tie. He looked as if Gemma had called him out on a medical emergency. "Sit down, please," he said coolly. We squeezed onto the sofa, sitting tightly together with our knees touching, like three nervous patients waiting to be told we had some incurable disease.

"Gemma was at school today when somebody told her they were looking forward to seeing her perform tomorrow night. Obviously, she had no idea what they were talking about. Until they showed her the leaflet."

He held up a tatty piece of blue paper, as if it was Exhibit A in some courtroom drama. "I can't imagine why you think you're ready to enter the Battle of the Bands," Martin continued scathingly.

"Well, we think we are," said CJ defiantly. "We think we can win."

Martin let out a hollow laugh.

"All I want to know is, why did you enter without telling me?" said Gemma in a trembling voice.

CJ, Daz and I looked at each other. This was not the plan at all! We were meant to wait until we'd finished the practice and then tell Gemma that the band wanted to move in a different musical direction; that her voice, as lovely as it was, just didn't suit the type of stuff we wanted to play; that we were very grateful to her and all that, but it was time to say goodbye.

"It was meant to be a surprise," I said lamely.

"It was certainly that," remarked Martin. "But why the subterfuge? If you wanted to enter, you could at least have given Gemma a say in the matter. You can't just expect someone to turn up and sing with only a day's notice."

"That's the whole point, Dad. They don't want me to sing," murmured Gemma.

"Yes, we do," I blurted out.

Daz and CJ gave me such an icy stare they could have frozen me to the spot.

"No, we don't," said Daz.

"We do, I mean we did, but we're moving in a new direction," blustered CJ, trying to revert to the original plan of action and making no sense at all.

"I really don't understand what's going on," Martin sighed. "Is Salamander a band or not?"

"Of course it is," I said.

"Then who is in charge?"

"We all are," I insisted. "It was my idea to start up, but we all make the decisions."

"Except me, obviously," said Gemma grimly.

I knew what she was thinking – that she had more talent in her little finger than the rest of us put together. For once, though, she didn't mention it. Maybe she was learning something from all this. I certainly was – like the next time I wanted to ditch a band member I would do it over the phone.

"So, what's happening tomorrow night?" asked Martin with feigned patience. "Is Salamander playing in the Battle of the Bands?"

"Yes!" said the three of us emphatically.

"Then I presume that you need Gemma to sing the vocals."

There was a pause.

"If you wanted to enter with a different line-up, you should have given yourself another name."

"Oh yeah, I suppose so," said Daz, who was easily dazzled by Martin's scheming logic.

"As to whether Gemma will still *want* to sing, well, that's up to her. How do you feel, darling?"

The three of us looked at her with bated breath. CJ and Daz wanted Gemma to refuse to have anything more to do with us, but I desperately wanted her to say yes. Partly because I felt we had been hard on her when she didn't totally deserve it, but mainly because "Don't Let Me Go" wouldn't sound right if CJ sang it. The song needed a girl's voice.

"All right, I'll sing," Gemma said finally. "But I don't want to practise tonight. I'm still in a state of shock."

Daz, CJ and I tramped home like the remnants of a defeated army. They were furious with me for "betraying them", and with themselves for allowing Gemma and her beloved daddy to get the better of us.

"We're so stupid! Why didn't we just call ourselves another name?" wailed Daz. "I never liked Salamander anyway."

"Perhaps we could enter under another name," said CJ hopefully.

"It's too late now," I insisted. "We've got to do the gig. I tell you, I'm going to surprise you tomorrow. I'm going to drum like I've never done before."

"Oh yeah?" scoffed CJ. "Well, I won't hold my breath."

9

It was the twenty-third of November.

I woke up feeling like a little boy on Christmas morning. My insides were churning with excitement, my heart beating just that little bit faster than usual. Tonight Salamander was going to give its first ever live performance – it was one for the record books, for music historians to note and remember. I thought about what CJ had said the night before: "We think we can win." Was it possible? Those words alone made me feel sick and light-headed, as if I'd just downed two pints of cheap cider on an empty stomach. This could be the beginning, the first step on the road to fame and success. I decided that the band needed to start its own scrapbook. I would buy one on the way to college that morning.

Why did I decide to go to college that day when I had been absent for so long? I'm not sure. Perhaps I needed to do something dull and boring to steady my nerves. I had slept with Murph's drumsticks alongside me in the bed, and they had given me a night of strange, troubled dreams – none of which, fortunately, I could remember.

College was much as I predicted. My Media Studies teacher raised her eyebrows when I loped into the room and said she'd assumed I'd given up the course. Had I seen any good films during my absence that I would like to give an analysis of? I hated sarcastic teachers more than anything. I shot her a filthy look and took a seat in the corner of the class, by the window. Within a few minutes, I was drifting off into a much-needed sleep.

At lunchtime, Daz, CJ and I discussed what we were going to wear for the gig, like a group of silly girls. CJ said image was important – we should wear ordinary clothes to give the impression that playing live gigs was no big deal.

"I bet Little Miss Muffet won't be wearing ordinary clothes," moaned Daz. "She'll probably turn up in a frigging ball gown."

"No, she won't," I reassured him. "But girls always dress up more than lads, you know that."

"Just make sure you're wearing something that shows a bit of attitude," added CJ, our self-appointed style consultant. "Ordinary, but not too boring."

We spent the rest of the day wandering in and out of the coffee bar and interrupting various classes, trying to drum up support. Daz reckoned that if we could get loads of skater dudes moshing and shouting it would help to drown out the sticky bits in the songs. It would also influence the judges into thinking that we already had a big following.

The excitement was building. Everywhere we went our friends shouted, "See you tonight. Scurvy Joe's, seven o'clock! Good luck!" People were surprised to learn that we had a band, and they seemed to look on us with new-found respect – of course, at that stage they hadn't heard us play.

I got home at about three o'clock in the afternoon. I was feeling sweaty with nerves and anticipation – CJ had told me that I badly needed a shower. Mum was still at work, Dad was out (I guessed he was drinking at the Grenadier) and Zoe was still at nursery school. I went into my bedroom and put Stride's tape into my stereo – for once, I was going to play it out loud, at full volume. I borrowed an extension lead from downstairs and positioned the machine just inside the bathroom – it meant leaving the door open, but, what the hell, I was on my own for once. I pressed *play*, then swiftly got undressed and stepped into the shower. The water was hot and stinging. I smothered myself in Mum's shower gel and lathered my body all over till I smelt like a giant strawberry. I sang along to the music at the top of my voice. I felt happy. For once in my life, everything was coming together. I looked through the frosted shower screen at my pile of clothes on the floor. I could see Murph's drumsticks lying on top of my jeans. Would it happen tonight? Would Murph's restless spirit slip into my world and join me on the drums? Surely it was an opportunity he couldn't resist. God only knows, I needed the help.

I stayed so long in the shower that the hot water ran out. It was getting late, and we'd been told to be at Scurvy Joe's by five for a soundcheck. There were heaps of bands playing – just one song in the first round. We had been debating which one to play first. If we started with our best song – "Don't Let Me Go" – we'd be giving ourselves a better chance of getting through to the next round. But then we'd be on a downhill slide with little chance of winning. On the other hand, if we started with our worst song we might get knocked out straightaway. It was a dilemma, and we hadn't really made up our minds yet. I was going over this problem in my mind as I dried myself, simultaneously humming along to a rather good guitar solo on the second to last track of the tape.

"Where the hell did you get that?"

I spun round. Dad was standing on the landing, his back leaning heavily against the wall. He looked pale with shock, as if he had just seen – or should I say heard – a ghost.

"I found it," I lied instantly, covering myself with the towel.

"Where?"

"In a shop."

"A shop?" he repeated slowly, as if it was a foreign word. "What, a music shop?"

"Sort of... It doesn't matter..."

There was a pause. He looked at me, and I looked at him. We were like two cowboys preparing for a gun battle.

"I know who it is," I said. "It's you and Mum, isn't it?"

He didn't respond, just carried on staring at me, his face hard and expressionless.

"Well? Isn't it?"

"Turn it off before she comes back," he said finally. "You'll give her a heart attack." Then he heaved himself off the wall and went downstairs. But if he thought he could make the problem disappear by walking away, he was wrong.

"I know all about it, Dad," I persisted, running downstairs after him, the bath towel wrapped around my waist. My wet hair was dripping onto my shoulders and running down my back in cold trickles. "I got the tape from Welly. He's told me everything."

Dad sat on the sofa and picked up *The Mirror*. He pretended to read the front page, but his eyes flickered when I mentioned Welly's name.

"I know all about Murph and how he died," I pressed. "I've been to his grave, and I've been to his house. I've met his mum. I've even played on his drum kit." That's when he suddenly sprang to life.

"You're talking shit, d'yer hear me? Shit!" Dad shouted. "Murph died over sixteen years ago. How could you play his kit? That's shit!"

"You never went to see her, did you?" I replied, standing right in front of him, half-naked and shivering. "Mrs Murphy – remember her? When you were a kid you were hardly ever out of her house. But when Murph died you just forgot her, left her on her own. If you'd bothered to keep in touch you'd know that she's kept his room just as it was – his bed, his posters, even his clothes are still lying on the chair. And his drums – they're still there, in the corner of the room. Remember? Red and silver with 'Stride' painted on the bass?"

"Why you doing this, Liam?" he asked, his voice no longer threatening, but quivering with rage. "What's it all about?"

"You gave me his name and you never even told me! It's stupid, Dad. All the time we're going around with these secrets. I've got secrets too, you know..."

He shot me a pained look and got up from the chair. There was a moment in which I thought he was going to hit me or push me to the ground, but he just stood there, trembling.

"We never talk!" I shouted. "We just argue and fight. I feel like you hate me. Why? Why do you hate me, Dad?"

"I don't," he replied. "I hate myself." He picked up his keys and left, shutting the front door with a quiet click. I heard him walk slowly down the front path, the car door opening, the engine spluttering into life and then rattling away into the distance. Who knows where he was going? I was standing in the middle of the lounge, barefoot and freezing cold, amazed by my own fearlessness. In sixteen years I'd never spoken to my dad like that.

Now he knew that I knew about Stride, but Mum didn't – that was crazy. I felt a strong urge to go and find her, but there wasn't time. I needed to get to Scurvy Joe's. I went back upstairs and got dressed. The tape had come to an end and was buzzing annoyingly in the machine. I removed it and took it downstairs to the kitchen, where I left it next to the kettle. It was clearly labelled *Stride Demo Tape* – Mum would know instantly what it was. By the time I returned from the Battle of the Bands, she would have recovered from the shock and maybe even have spoken to Dad. It would work out all right. I prayed to the non-existent God that it would work out all right – for Mum's sake, if nobody else's.

By the time I made it to Scurvy Joe's, CJ, Daz and Gemma were already there, an awkward-looking trio. I was surprised that Daddy hadn't come along, too, but Gemma told me that Martin was on call.

"What a shame," whispered CJ sarcastically in my ear.

The place was in chaos. Twelve bands needed to soundcheck in two hours – it was virtually impossible. There was gear lying about all over the place. Some bands had insisted on bringing extra pieces of kit. Everyone seemed to have tons more stuff than we did. Leads twisted across the room like black snakes, tripping people over and forming themselves inexplicably into knots; there were empty guitar cases strewn all over the floor; three drummers were arguing about the height of the cymbals; and everyone was complaining about the lack of stage space.

"There's nothing I can do about it," insisted red-faced Charlie, the organizer. "We need to pack as many people in as we can. All this sound and lighting gear cost a bomb to hire, you know." He pointed at a high stack of enormous amps at either side of the narrow stage. The drum kit that we all had to use was wedged uncomfortably between them. The amps looked powerful enough to play Wembley. Our hopes of the audience drowning out our dodgy bits faded in an instant.

A metal bar had been fixed across the ceiling and several heavy-duty stage lights hung down from it, right above where I would be sitting. It was going to be hot and sweaty up there, with coloured lights flashing in our faces and the bass amp thumping in our chests. I couldn't wait. I hoped somebody had brought a camera. We needed a photo of our first gig for the Salamander scrapbook.

Charlie drew our names out of a hat to see which order we were going to play. "It saves arguments," he explained, having organized several of these competitions before. We were drawn second to last, which CJ reckoned was the best possible position.

"It's like being the headline band!" he said.

"Won't they be bored by the time they get to us?" I argued. "If the other bands are crap, they might go home."

"Nah, they'll be warmed up nicely," said CJ. "But it means we'd better play our fastest song – 'Don't Let Me Go'." Gemma and Daz agreed it was the right decision, and I wasn't going to argue. In my heart, it was what I'd wanted to play all along. I gripped Murph's drumsticks tightly in my pocket. I felt that he was there with me, giving me support, bringing us luck.

The doors opened just after seven and the audience filed in. Within minutes the room was heaving with kids. I'd never seen the place so packed and Gemma remarked that they must be in breach of fire regulations.

If only she would keep her mouth shut, I thought to myself, I could really fancy that girl. She was looking surprisingly fit – she had sprayed glitter in her hair and was wearing dark red lipstick. To Daz's relief she wasn't wearing a ball gown, just a pair of widely flared jeans and a lacy top. I was glad we hadn't been able to dump her. We were the only line-up with a female vocalist and it gave us a bit of individuality.

Every band seemed to have brought its own crowd of supporters who shoved and pushed their way to the front to cheer in their friends' faces. The change-overs on stage were fast and furious, and the corresponding movements in the crowd became quite aggressive. Waves of kids barged their way forward, kicking their opponents out of the way. I couldn't see how they could tell which band was playing: they all sounded exactly the same – heavy power chords and lots of mindless thrashing about on the drums. The singers screeched into the microphones and several of them complained that they couldn't hear themselves.

"They need voice training!" Gemma shouted at me. "They'll damage their vocal chords if they're not careful."

I was feeling really sick by now. I hadn't been able to eat any tea and I'd been drinking lager. The place was unbearably hot and I was developing a headache. I started to wonder if I might be coming down with flu, but it was just nerves. I couldn't see Welly anywhere, although it was hard to tell in the mayhem. Why hadn't he turned up? All I needed was a wave or a thumbs-up in support. And surely he wanted to hear us play "Don't Let Me Go"? There was no time to look for him properly. It was our turn next, and we were huddling at the side of the stage, waiting to leap into action. The posh boys' band was on before us, playing some poncy song about animal experiments. The little curly-haired drummer was beating the life out of the skins, but for once he didn't make me feel like a complete no-hoper. Tonight was going to be different. I had Murph on my side.

"On you get, no mucking about, we're behind schedule as it is," shouted Charlie, virtually pushing us on stage.

Gemma went straight to the front and adjusted the microphone, while CJ plugged in and gave his guitar a rough tune. Daz sat himself down at the keyboards and took a deep breath. Our mates forced their way to the front, pushing and swearing at everyone else to get out of the way. CJ had told them to start moshing straight-away because the song was short and we couldn't afford to hang around. I sat down on the drum stool and took out Murph's sticks. My hands were slippery with fear and sweat. I wiped them on my trousers, realizing why the kid before me had been wearing gloves.

"Hello, everyone!" called out Gemma, waving excitedly at her friends. "We're going to play a song for you called 'Don't Let Me Go'. It's a cover actually, but I think you'll find it's very different—"

"Just get on with it!" someone shouted from the crowd.

"Come on, Murph," I whispered quietly. "Let's do it." Then I shouted, "One–two–three–four!" I couldn't wait for Murph to decide whether to join me or not – I just had to start. CJ played the opening riff, Daz came in only a bar late on the intro and, before I knew it, we were a third of the way into the song.

The noise was deafening. All I could hear were the

drums crashing and thumping around my ears and vibrating through my ribcage. Gemma was singing her little heart out, but I could barely catch a word. For all I knew we might be playing four separate songs. I just kept counting, my eyes on the drums, my feet banging away at the pedal, trying to concentrate ... and all the time wondering if it was Murph playing, or me? I didn't feel the same surge of weird energy that I had experienced in his bedroom, although my arms were aching as before. Maybe it was the drum kit itself that his spirit inhabited; maybe it had nothing to do with the sticks. I didn't know, and I didn't have time to think about it.

The crowd was moshing like crazy in front of us. It was mental! They charged into each other, jumping upwards and sideways at the same time, their heads shaking, their bodies heaving. Then some of the lads started climbing on each other's shoulders and hurling themselves forward onto people's heads.

"I just want to be with you, but you want to let me go!" screeched Gemma above the din, no doubt damaging her vocal chords in the process. *"I can't stand this situation, my life's full of complication, I just want to stay with you, but you want to let me go!"*

CJ went into his guitar solo, but he seemed to have forgotten the chords. He jumped up in the air to compensate, and the lead fell out of his guitar. While he struggled to put it back in, Daz improvised on the keyboard. It sounded completely crap, but nobody in the audience seemed to notice or care. They started to surge towards us in a massive tidal wave of bodies. Gemma cried out and backed into the drum kit as about thirty kids landed on the stage in a heap.

"Get back! Get back!" I shouted, but the bodies kept coming forward. I was trapped behind the kit and couldn't escape. Two idiots had climbed up one of the amplifier towers and were swinging off the lighting bar. Suddenly, the other stack wobbled and the top amplifier crashed to the floor, narrowly missing Daz but smashing straight onto the keyboard. The stage was engulfed with people. It was mad. CJ turned and screamed at me. He had a look of absolute horror on his face. The very next moment something sharp and heavy fell and hit me on the back of the head, knocking me forward onto the kit. I remember opening my eyes for a second and seeing the tom skin covered in sticky red blood. Then I lost consciousness.

First, there was a period of quiet darkness, like plunging into a deep, sudden sleep. It probably only lasted for a few seconds, but I was already in the place that Welly had told me about – where Time didn't exist. I could feel the Past, Present and Future meeting and embracing, like old friends. And I was weaving in and out of them in a dance, briefly taking their hands before moving on. My mind became full of the most colourful images – it was like watching a video diary of my life, except the events were all in the wrong order, jumping backwards and forwards in time.

Yet these were not the edited highlights of my existence – this wasn't the Best of Liam Condie. They were just everyday scenes, ordinary moments that I'd randomly captured and stored in my brain. I was as a toddler playing in the front garden – then I was a baby crying in a pushchair. Suddenly, I pressed fast-forward and was kissing some girl I'd met at a party a year before. Then I rewound to see Mum dishing up mashed potato in the kitchen of our old house. Forward again, and I was standing at a bus stop, holding a bunch of flowers. Then back several years to see myself playing football in the street with Daz and CJ. There were other pictures, hundreds of them, but they flashed through my head too quickly for me to recognize. I felt dizzy and sick, utterly disorientated. I tried to call out "Stop!" But my throat was dry and no words would come. I begged for the pictures to fade or slow down at least. I wanted peace, silence, rest...

Then suddenly, the image I was seeing remained fixed. And it wasn't from the past – it was from the present. It was happening right now, at Scurvy Joe's. A small group of people was clustered together on the wrecked stage. I could make out the glitter in Gemma's hair, the bright blue of CJ's T-shirt. Daz was standing to one side, breathing heavily, his face as white as a sheet. There was no music, just a dull rhythmic murmur, punctuated by the odd shout of urgency and the cries of girls sobbing. Red-faced, bleary-eyed teenagers were being ushered out into the street. The dance floor was littered with cigarette packets and empty cans, broken glass, a couple of lost beanies, a forgotten bag, a dis-carded jumper...

I realized that I was watching all this from some high vantage point, as if I was sitting on the ceiling – except the room didn't seem to have a ceiling any more. I was floating in the air, many feet above the ground, and nobody could see me. They were all looking down at the floor. A couple of people were crouching around something. A girl stepped forward and offered her coat.

"Everyone, leave – leave now," said a voice below. "You're only in the way."

I heard the distant sound of an ambulance siren gradually getting louder and closer. The cluster of people drew back. And there was my body, lying on the floor next to the drum kit. It wasn't moving or making a sound. The back of my head was oozing blood, like thick red wine. My spirit felt a sudden wrench, a stretching – a tearing apart. I had an overwhelming longing to reunite with my body and yet knew I was utterly powerless. I could sense myself being dragged backwards, upwards and out of reach. The scene below was becoming more and more distant, till the figures – and among them my own precious body – were nothing but tiny dots on the ground.

I was dying ... dying and drifting away.

rewind ◄◄

10

I must have made a long journey that night. I remember the beginning – the terrible feeling of being wrenched from my body – and I remember the end. But what happened in the middle remains a mystery. At some point I slipped out of my own world and entered another – several others, I believe. Yet the moment of departure was lost to me. Did I knock on a door and beg for it to be opened? Or did I scream with protest as a hand took hold of me and dragged me through a gap in the clouds? It was hard to know for sure – those first days were a mass of contradictions and confusion. But I do not believe I met that great, white-bearded man in the sky. Nor were there other spirits to guide me along the way. I was entirely on my own.

It was like slipping in and out of an endless dream. Vivid images would swirl before me and then plunge into blackness, spinning me into a deep sleep. My spirit soon longed for those periods of dark forgetfulness, of utter nothingness. But they were all too brief. Suddenly I would be roused into consciousness again. I would find myself sitting in the swaying branches of a tall tree, floating in a rowing boat on a calm, clear ocean or being hurled through a raging storm. No image or sensation lasted long – entire worlds flashed past me in a second, like glimpses from a speeding train. There was a sense of urgency, as if I was constantly being hurried along to the next destination, but I felt no danger. No fiends or monsters were chasing me – I wasn't running away from anyone or anything. I was not afraid. Just exhausted and bewildered.

And what substance was I now made of? Did I have any shape at all? I was still able to see but somehow had no eyes. I could hear the wind rushing round my head but seemed to have no ears. I could smell sea water and burning wood, I could feel my legs brushing against the leaves of a tree, but I could neither see nor touch my own body. I wondered whether I was simply calling up memories of being alive – like a man who has gone blind but can still remember what it is like to see, or someone who has lost his legs but can recall the sensation of walking. I began to worry that these memories would fade and, before long, I would be a senseless blob of matter floating through the universe, without perception or understanding. But then, I thought – surprising myself that I could still think – perhaps *that* is the oblivion my spirit longs for. Maybe I should let go of the memories and submit myself to the eternal nothingness. But it seemed that I could not. I was still fighting, resisting, wandering through the spirit world, searching to find a place that I could understand.

And eventually, after days or years or centuries, even,

I found it. I woke from one of those long passages of dark, unknowing sleep and, for the first time, felt stillness. I had come to rest. Thankfully, I was not sitting on a puffy cloud playing a harp. I was right back in my home town, where I had been born and where I had lived my short, uneventful life.

I found myself – I'll never know how I got there – sitting on a low wall outside an unfamiliar house. I had probably walked down this street before or seen it from the top of a bus, but I couldn't place it. I guessed that I was in Corsfield, the older, highest part of the town, where my grandparents and Mary Murphy lived. I could see the spire of what was probably St Cedd's in the distance to my right. A pink-grey dawn was breaking over the crowded horizon. There was no mistaking the view. This was my ordinary, boring town with its tatty estates, its crumbling tower blocks and graffiti covered walls. And somewhere down there was my house in that dead-end street where I had felt – often with a sigh of disappointment – that I belonged.

I traced imaginary steps in my head – through the Madeley Estate, past the pub, down the alleyway and round the bend into Meadow Walk. There was number twenty-six: the short path, weeds in the front garden, glass door, my key turning in the lock, two steps down the narrow hallway, climbing the stairs leading up to my bedroom, my bed, my pillow, my pale blue sheets... How I wanted to lie on those sheets and close my eyes. It would feel so good to be back home. And after I'd had a good rest, I would hop on the bus and ride into the town centre. I'd sit on the steps outside the library and wait for my mates to turn up. "CJ, Daz, it's been ages! How you doing? Missed me, have you? What happened at the Battle of the Bands? Did we win?"

But I couldn't do that, could I? All that had passed. Something had fallen on my head and changed everything. I was here, and yet I was not here... I was dead.

Did that mean I was a ghost? Was I condemned to spend the rest of eternity wandering round my old haunts, a shadowy figure that jumped out and said boo to people on dark winter nights? The thought made me laugh, and I discovered that I could hear myself... Or was that just the memory of laughter? I laughed again and said my name out loud several times. My voice sounded unfamiliar and hesitant, as if I was learning to speak after a long silence. I tried whispering, then shouting, then bellowing – a low, long cry. This was not memory; this was happening now!

And then I realized that I could see my body. It had returned to me – legs, feet, toes, chest, arms. I found that I had hands again and lifted them to my face. I felt my eyes, my mouth – lips, teeth and tongue. I traced the shape of my nose, the hollow of my cheekbones. My cheeks were soft, but the sides of my face were rough from my half-hearted attempts at shaving. There were no new bristles on my chin. I felt the back of my head. It was tender but, to my relief, not bleeding. Unsurprisingly, I was still wearing the clothes from the gig – the ordinary clothes that CJ had insisted we wore to prove that it was not a special occasion. Had I known that I was going to wear this old T-shirt and jeans until the end of time, I think I might have chosen something a bit more exciting. I may be dead, I thought, but I haven't lost my sense of humour.

The road was empty. It was very early in the morning and not even the milkman had come round yet. An old car drove past me, but the driver was looking ahead and didn't notice me. I needed to know whether I was visible, whether anybody could hear me speak. I was solid to my own touch, but a living person might see me as a grey shadow or a floating mist. They might be able to put a hand right through my body. And what powers might I have now? Could I walk through walls? Could I fly? Now, there was an interesting thought. Maybe I could jump off buildings or hurl myself in front of cars without being hurt. Then I remembered the soreness at the back of my head and touched it again. No, I could still feel pain. I decided not to risk doing anything stupid. Being a ghost was extraordinary enough – there was no need to get carried away.

The first place I wanted to see was home. I longed to find my mum, and Zoe – even Dad would be a welcome sight now. I wondered how they had taken my death. I conjured up an inner vision of Mum, her eyes red with crying as she followed my coffin to the cemetery. I imagined her weeping at my graveside, bringing fresh flowers each day and scrubbing the inscription with a toothbrush, just like Mary Murphy. Then I banished the scene from my mind. I didn't want my mum to be like that, obsessed with grief. But neither did I want her to have forgotten me completely. The thought of peering through the windows of my house to see every-body laughing and relaxing in front of the television suddenly frightened me.

But ghosts have to haunt somewhere, I argued, walking down the hill in the direction of the town centre. And there must be a reason why I'd come back. Not everyone returns from the dead; otherwise the world would be jam-packed with spirits, wafting about, getting in each other's way. There must be some unfinished business, some question that needs answering. Isn't that what being a ghost is all about? Weird Welly would know, I muttered under my breath. He'd be able to explain it. Then I stopped in my silent tracks. I suddenly remembered what he had said to me the night before the gig, when he had stood up and hugged me so tightly, so strangely.

"Whatever happens, you mustn't be afraid…"

Welly had known all along that I was about to die! That was why he hadn't turned up to the Battle of the Bands, because he couldn't bear to witness it. Maybe one of his old people ghosts had told him about it. Or maybe he guessed that Murph's spirit had come to guide me through the Valley of Death… But I instantly dismissed that idea. I hadn't once felt Murph's presence on my strange journey. I had been alone, utterly alone. I began to feel angry with Welly. Christ, I thought, he might have told me what was going to happen. He might have stopped me going to the gig! I probably wouldn't have believed him but he could have at least tried.

"Come and find me. I'll be there," he'd said.

Well, I was going to take him at his word. I had plenty to say to him, too. His shop was a good thirty minutes' walk away, but it didn't bother me. I had all the time in the world.

As I carried on walking, the day grew lighter. It seemed warmer than November, more like a cool summer morning. People were emerging from their houses, getting into their cars, waiting at bus stops. But they didn't look quite the same as I expected. I couldn't put my finger on it, but something wasn't right. This was my town but it was also somewhere else. Nobody seemed to notice me, but then I had often had the experience of feeling invisible, so I tried dancing along the pavement, waving my arms in the air and shouting. There was no reaction from anybody, no discreet turning of the head, not one lingering glance. It was a bit alarming, this being here and yet not here. But it was also liberating. For once I could say and do as I wished and nobody could stop me. I started swearing my head off, making rude gestures at passers-by – it was fantastic. I thought of all the people I didn't like – friends who had betrayed me, girlfriends who had dumped me, teachers who had humiliated me, guys in shops who had refused to sell me a measly can of beer. I was going to hunt them down one by one and finally get my own back. But then, I thought, if they can't see or hear me, if they can't feel my blows, what would be the point? A secret revenge would be no revenge at all. I wrestled with this latest realization as I followed the railway track towards the station. Welly would understand. He would work it all out. I was sure that he would be able to *hear* me at least, in the same way that he heard the old people that sat in his shop and burbled into the small hours. If he could *see* me, too, that would be all the better. I was furious with Welly for not trying to save my life but, now I was dead, he was my only hope.

I turned the corner and walked down the filthy back-street that led to Welly's place. It was at the end of a row of disused workshops and boarded-up shops. I had been there so many times that my feet could take me there without me thinking. And yet it all looked so unfamiliar. I reached the end of the street and stopped.

So, why was his shop not there? It should've been right there! But instead, on the same corner at the same junction of the same two roads was a plumber's mer-chants. The window was crammed with toilet bowls and sinks, shiny taps, swivelling shower heads, and a little wall of pink tiles. Where was all the junk? Where was the mystical stuff? And most important of all – where was Weird Welly? I stood on the pavement and stared at the display, willing and wishing it would sud-denly transform into a pile of smelly mattresses and broken garden furniture.

Was this a parallel universe, in which most things were the same but for some rather crucial, not to say irritating, changes? I looked further down the street. The "disused" workshop was opening its gates, and two of the shops weren't boarded up at all. One was a barber's and the other a newsagent's. Maybe I had moved into a different Time altogether? I had to buy a paper to see the date. No, no, not buy a paper. I would never have to buy another thing in my ... I was going to say "life". But I could find a way to describe my new-found state later. Right now I had to see a paper. I ran to the shop and tried the door. The sign said OPEN but I couldn't push it. I could touch things but not move them, nor make any impression on them. The new physical laws of ghostliness were starting to become clear, and they were extremely frustrating. I would have to wait until somebody came along and opened the door for me.

Time was meaningless to me now, and yet knowing the date was crucial. Several minutes passed before somebody came along, but they walked straight past the shop and disappeared round the corner. I leant against the shop window and tapped my foot impatiently. How many years had passed since my death? A couple? Five? Ten? Could it be as many as twenty? Was Welly even still alive himself? I shuddered at the thought. I needed to see him, to talk to him. He would help me complete my "unfinished business" – at the very least, he may be able to tell me what that business was.

Finally, a young woman walked towards me, wearing office clothes and carrying a large handbag. As she reached the door of the shop, she stopped and looked behind her, as if aware that somebody was watching her. She looked down the empty street, even glanced up at the windows for a face behind a curtain. I was sure she could feel my presence because she suddenly shivered, drawing her jacket across her chest. After a few seconds she decided it was nothing and shrugged me off, but I took it as a hopeful sign. If Welly was no longer around, there would be others. It was just a matter of tracking them down.

The woman pushed open the door and I followed her into the shop. There was a fat pile of morning papers on the counter. I stood close behind her and watched the goose bumps rise on her neck as she paid for a bar of chocolate and a box of matches. I craned over her shoulder to look at the date on the front page...

Surely this couldn't be right.

It was Friday 13 June 1986 – six months before the date of my birth.

11

It took some time for the discovery to sink in. So, I was here and yet not here... I was dead and yet unborn.

I sat on the floor in a daze, leaning against a rack of sweets and chocolate bars, my legs outstretched across the aisle, my feet resting lightly on a shelf of tissue boxes and bottles of shampoo. A plasterer came in, leaving strange white footprints as he crossed the floor. He was covered from head to toe in dirty white powder, and his hair was matted with cobwebs and plaster dust. I had to say he made a far more convincing ghost than I did. He paid for his can and walked towards me. I was about to withdraw my legs, when he calmly stepped over them and went on his way! This happened again and again. Big, gruff builders, car mechanics in greasy overalls, a yawning postman – men whose work was rooted in real things, who built and mended and delivered – trudged into the shop one after the other and stepped over my outstretched legs. It was as if a small part of their beings was aware of my presence; a little-used section in their brains could detect and respond to the supernatural. I was tempted to sit there all day to see if I could find the one person that was completely insensitive to my ghostly presence, but I had more pressing things to do. Unfinished business.

I needed to find Welly. He would be about my own age – a lad who had never met me, but whom I already knew pretty well. That was why he behaved as if I was an old friend when I turned up at his shop. He already knew my story – he'd heard it long ago. Because what was about to happen had already taken place. The Past, Present and Future were intertwined. They could not be separated and made to stand in a neat line – beginning, then middle, then end. Welly knew what he was talking about from personal experience.

"Poor kid," I muttered to myself. No wonder he turned out weird.

Where would I find him? That was my immediate problem. I knew he had lived in Corsfield as a lad, near Murph and my parents – "we were at school together," he'd told me. But were they still at school? And was Murph still alive? I racked my brains to remember the date on his grave. It was the same year but what month and what day? I had read that inscription so many times, had chanted it over and over in my head in a clumsy attempt to communicate with Murph's spirit, and now I couldn't for the "life" of me remember the actual bloody date! I decided that it was July, or maybe June – I played with different combinations of month and number until my brain went into spasm. They all seemed to sound right.

There was only one way to settle the issue of Murph's

life or death status, and that was to go to his house and find out. It was also the only place that I knew Welly definitely visited. Surely if I hung around long enough he would eventually turn up. At last I had something resembling a plan.

It was a long hike back up the hill to Corsfield. The weather was warm and I soon discovered that, while spirits do not need to eat or drink, they tire easily. So, just as I had done when I was alive, I took the number 95 bus, surprised to find that it was still running the same route. I stood at the front of the queue and hopped on as soon as the doors opened. Free rides from now on. I laughed to myself. It was the morning rush hour. People were on their way to factories and offices, and kids were going to school. The bus was already packed, so I had to stand.

The same thing happened. People stood very close to me but did not touch. It must have looked as if there was an empty space where I was standing – a small area that nobody would enter. Some tiny part of their subconscious knew I was there. It reminded me of a few occasions when I had travelled on a crowded train. People had stood in between the cars and leant against the doors, and yet there had often been the odd empty seat that nobody wanted to sit in. I looked around the bus for similar gaps, wondering whether other ghosts might be taking the same journey. But the rest of the gangway was tightly packed, right through to the back. Then I wondered whether I had the ability to see ghosts – maybe they looked ordinary and solid to me. I started to stare at people, searching for fellow travellers on the ethereal plane, but from the bored expressions on their faces it seemed unlikely.

I spotted a tiny girl wearing a neat school uniform, bumping about on her mother's lap as the bus swung heavily around a roundabout. She was smiling at me! She could see me – I was sure of it. This was a complete breakthrough. I felt elated. I lifted my hand and gave her a small, gentle wave. She waved back. I pulled a silly face, pulling at my ears and sticking out my tongue. She giggled!

"What's so funny?" asked her mother irritably, pulling her jacket from under the girl's bottom. "Sit still, will you!"

"It's that man," she whispered.

The woman looked up and stared blankly in my direction.

"What man?"

"Him. There! He's waving at me."

"Don't start all that again," she snapped. "There's nobody there."

I got off at the right stop for once and made my way to Murph's house. It was only about nine o'clock. If Murph was still at school or had a job he would have already left. If not, he would probably still be in bed. The prospect of hanging around in his front garden all day did not appeal to me. I wasn't even sure that he was still alive. I was about to embark on a gruesome mission to the churchyard to see if a fresh grave had been dug, when Mary Murphy opened the front door to put the milk bottles out.

I gasped. This was the first person that I recognized from my own Time. She was herself and yet not herself. She looked a lot younger, of course. Her hair was a deep brown colour, almost black, and her face was calm and contented. This was not the expression of someone who had just lost her only beloved son. There were no lines of sadness around her mouth, no look of weary grief in her eyes. It was an ordinary Friday morning and she had just finished washing up the breakfast things. Mrs Murphy glanced up at the clear blue sky and decided she would wash the bed linen... At least, that was what I imagined she was thinking. She went back inside and got on with her housework. I sat down on the neatly mown front lawn and considered the "facts".

Here I was, a spirit from the Future – if you looked at the situation from Welly's perspective – with precious information. For a start, I knew that one of his friends was about to die in a car accident. I could even tell him the exact date, if I could bloody well remember it. I also knew that his band was going to split up, that Mary Murphy would go mad with grief, that my parents were going to have a horribly unhappy marriage, that my dad was going to end up as an unemployable slob and that Welly would turn into a lonely wizard who lived in a junk shop. Oh yes, and that my teenage mother was pregnant. I was hardly an angel bringing glad tidings of great joy.

So why was I here? What was this unfinished business? Maybe I was meant to stop Murph dying and transform everyone's future. It had certainly been Murph's death that had destroyed their hopes and dashed all their chances. If Murph had lived, if Stride had got its recording contract and become rich and famous, what difference would that have made to my existence? Maybe I would have been brought up in California, or in some huge mansion in the countryside, attending some trendy posh school with a load of other rock stars' kids. And I would never have played football in some scummy street with CJ and Daz, or had to eat fish fingers and lumpy mashed potato, or sat on the cold concrete steps outside the library and had the dumb idea to form a band. And maybe, just maybe, I wouldn't have died on stage in Scurvy Joe's, smashed over the head by some sharp, heavy object – probably a stage light.

I had a sudden image of those two goons swinging off the lighting bar, the horrified expression on CJ's face... I shuddered and felt the tender part at the back of my head. There was no point in going over all that. I had to concentrate – think it all through. This was important stuff and I had to get it right. I was going to meet Welly soon and I had to decide how much he needed to know. I certainly couldn't stop Murph dying without his help.

Then, without any warning, a sudden swathe of darkness overcame me, and I fell asleep. It was deep and dreamless and I wanted it to last forever. When I woke up, I was still in Murph's front garden, but the whole atmosphere was different. I did not need a newspaper to tell me that this was not the same day. But I had no idea how much time had slipped by in my absence. I could even have floated further back into the past. It was hot and sticky, although the sun was no longer shining. Instead, the sky was a relentless grey, and it was pouring with rain. Only, the rain didn't touch me, as if it, too, sensed my presence and preferred to fall around my body. I became desperate to feel wetness on my skin. But when I reached out to touch the drops of water they escaped me. I tried to trick the rain, weaving my hand swiftly through the air, but it darted out of my way and I remained totally dry.

Then I heard music – a guitar, a girl singing, the steady beat of the drums. Stride was playing upstairs in Murph's bedroom. It was a track from the demo tape – the third song on the first side. I could hear it quite clearly through the open window. I remembered Mary Murphy telling me that she always made the band play with the windows shut, so as not to disturb the neighbours. Perhaps she was out.

I gazed up at the bedroom. So that's where they were – Sheryl and Garry, two sixteen-year-old lovers soon to plunge into marital hell, and poor Murph, drumming away, blissfully unaware that his days on earth were numbered. I felt overcome with impatient curiosity. I wanted to climb the drainpipe and peer through the window to look at them. But I'd never done such a thing in my wimpy life, and I wasn't about to start now. Besides, it was good to stand in the rainless rain and listen to them playing. I felt connected to them through the music, comforted by its familiarity. I was almost at peace. I hummed along with the tune, even sang some of the words quietly under my breath. The song sounded the same, and yet it was different. But this wasn't another contradiction for me to wrestle with. There was no keyboard sound, that was all. Which meant that Welly wasn't there. Just my bloody luck, I thought – just my bloody luck.

Then I saw him, scurrying towards me along the pavement, a large rectangular object in a black leather case tucked precariously under his arm. He had no coat on and was drenched through. His thick dark eyebrows were frowning in concentration. He was trying to run as fast as he could without dropping his keyboard. There was no avoiding him – no time to hide and, unfortunately, I could not zap myself into invisibility. Those people who made horror films had got the whole idea of ghosts completely round their neck – we were pretty pathetic creatures with no useful powers at all.

Welly stopped at the front door and rang the bell several times, panting for breath. His short dark hair was pasted against his skull, and rain water was dripping down his spotty adolescent face. It was Welly, and it was not Welly. I missed the knowing look in his watery green eyes, his wild, straggly hair, the ring through his nose that made him look like a prize bullock, his long, sweeping cloak and leather boots. This younger version looked fresh and overanxious. He was late for the practice and they had started without him. He began thumping on the door and shouting through the letterbox.

"Oi, let me in, will you? Someone!" He turned to me in search of sympathy. "They can't frigging hear me," he said. "Why won't his mum let me in?"

"I think she's gone out," I replied.

"Who are you?" He scanned my features, as if searching through the files of innumerable faces that he had glimpsed once and stored away in his brain. "Have I seen you before?"

"I don't think so," I answered carefully, no longer taking anything for granted. I knew all about those mischievous Beginnings, Middles and Ends, constantly jumping in front of one another, making me confused.

"I'm glad you can see me, Welly. I was worried you might not."

He frowned.

"Who are you?" he repeated, more seriously this time. "How come you're calling me that name?"

"I'm a friend... I know you, but you don't know me."

"I wish they'd answer the bloody door," he moaned, ringing again.

"Welly? I need to talk to you," I began cautiously. "Can we go somewhere? Looks like you could do with getting out of the rain."

Then he realized what it was that was so strange about me. I wasn't a grey shadow or a wafting mist. I simply wasn't wet. Welly stared at me, open-mouthed and a little frightened.

"The rain doesn't want to touch me," I explained.

"That's weird," he said, and I laughed. Things were going to get a whole lot weirder for young Pete Llewellyn and no mistake.

12

We sat in the corner of McDonald's – not the one by the library because it didn't exist. This was a different one at the other end of the High Street. Welly devoured a Big Mac while he listened to me explaining that I was, in fact, a ghost: a spirit from the other side, a spectre, a spook, a phantom or, to put it bluntly, a freshly dead person. None of this news seemed to put him off his burger, although his mouth kept dropping open in astonishment, revealing bits of chewed-up gherkin and tomato relish. It was not a pretty sight. How he must have looked to the other customers I don't know. As far as they were concerned, Welly was sitting on his own, gawping at an empty chair. I had to keep reminding him that the vast majority of the human race couldn't see me and that he should keep his voice down before somebody carted him off to the nearest mental hospital.

"Tell me something," I said. "What day is it today?"

"Tuesday," he whispered.

I counted on my fingers. "June seventeenth – does that sound right to you?"

"Yeah, it's something like that. This isn't a wind-up, is it? You are a real ghost?"

I sighed... Young Welly was proving to be hard work.

"Look," I said, "I'll prove it to you." I stood up and walked over to the queue of people waiting to order their Happy Meals and Chicken McNuggets. I did silly walks and pulled faces. I climbed onto the counter and danced. I shouted and swore and told the staff that they were conspiring with the capitalist system to keep the Third World in dire poverty. Welly was duly impressed by my daring. At one point he applauded and laughed out loud, which led to some raised eyebrows at the adjacent table.

"OK, satisfied now?" I said rather irritably as I returned to my seat. I was strangely exhausted by my short performance.

"So ... when did you ... er, pass over?" he whispered cautiously, not wanting to cause offence.

"November the twenty-third, 2002."

Welly's jaw dropped, and a lump of chewed-up sesame seed bun loomed into view.

"I'm from the Future – your future, that is. For me, I'm in the Past. In this Time, I haven't even been born yet."

"Nah, you've lost me there," said Welly. "That doesn't make sense—"

"None of it makes sense," I retorted. "You think I'm enjoying this? You think I want to be dead?"

"No, sorry ... I didn't mean to... It's just hard to get my head round it."

He ate his French fries, one by one, licking his fingers every couple of mouthfuls.

"So, how come you chose me to, er … you know, to reveal yourself to?"

I was asking the very same question myself.

"You're the only person I know that has psychic powers," I said.

Welly smiled, his chest puffing up. "I've got psychic powers?" he repeated grandly. "Cor, I never knew that."

"Hasn't anything strange happened to you before? Haven't you ever felt a cold blast of air or felt something brush past you or heard someone sighing in an empty room?"

"Nope," he said cheerfully. "Should I have done?"

"No, I just thought you might have had some previous experience, that's all. Some kind of inkling that you were a bit different from other people."

"Not that I can remember… Psychic powers, eh?"

"I've a lot to tell you, Welly," I said. "You'd better get yourself another drink. This could take some time."

And so I found myself giving Welly a crash course in Time concepts, explaining about Beginnings, Middles and Ends and how they misbehaved in the cosmos – theories that he had taught me himself. It was getting horribly confusing. Was I the one who had started him off on all this magic, occult stuff? Obviously, wimpy young Pete Llewellyn had never dabbled in the black arts – he wouldn't know a Ouija board if it hit him over the head. It was like that age-old problem – which came first, the chicken or the egg? Maybe that was how the conundrum came about in the first place. It was those Beginnings, Middles and Ends' faults. Just look at all the confusion they had caused, all the scientific research and philosophical debate. Welly was certainly bewildered by it. I had the distinct impression that his first lesson in quantum physics (if that indeed was what it was) was not sinking in. As he slurped up his Coke, his feeble brain diverted onto another, more practical track.

"So," he said, belching down a mouthful of fizz. "If you're from the Future, you must know who wins the World Cup."

It was my turn to drop a jaw in astonishment.

"What's that got to do with anything?"

"We're right in the middle of it! England play Paraguay tomorrow for a place in the quarter-finals. You tell me who wins, and I'll place a bet – my dad will have to do it for me. He won't mind – he's always gambling. We could win a fortune! Come on, then, who wins? If you could give me the exact score, that would be even better."

"I haven't—"

"And who wins the whole thing? No, don't tell me, let me guess… Italy? Or Brazil? Don't tell me it's West Germany!"

"I haven't the faintest idea," I replied. "I don't like football."

"Don't like football?"

"No. It's all about money: players getting paid millions of pounds, kids in Asia stitching up leather footballs for a few measly pence. It's not sport any more, it's just big business."

He looked dumbfounded. "But most people, ordinary people, they still watch football?"

"Yes, yes, of course. Most lads of my age are obsessed. Kevs particularly."

I looked at him, wondering. Was Welly a Kev? His hair wasn't cropped and he wasn't wearing designer sportswear. But he seemed to have the mentality of a Kev, although, to be fair, not many of them played the keyboards. I was taken aback by this terrifying possibility. What a punishment, to die and find myself haunting a Kev...

"So who's top of the First Division – in your time?" Welly continued with tedious curiosity. "Liverpool? Everton?"

"I don't even know what teams are in the First Div," I said wearily. "I expect Manchester United are top of the Premiership. They usually are."

"What's the Premiership?"

"It's above the First Division."

"No way! They've changed it then, have they? When did they do that?"

"Look, do we have to talk about football?"

"OK," said Welly thoughtfully. "Who wins the Grand National? The Men's Singles at Wimbledon?"

I shrugged.

"Formula One World Championship? Snooker? The US Open? The Tour de frigging France?"

"I'm sorry, I don't know... I'm not into sport, just music."

"All right, then, who wins the Eurovision Song Contest?"

"I just said, I'm into music!" I retorted sarcastically.

There was an awkward pause while Welly sucked on his straw.

"Ireland used to win it a lot, but I couldn't tell you which years. I'm not into any of that, Welly. I'm a peace-loving skater-dude."

"You go skating?" Welly pulled a face. "What, ice-skating?"

"No, skateboarding, you dork."

"Skateboarding? That went out years ago!" he scoffed. "It was a really big thing for a couple of years, then everyone gave up. Nobody could do it properly – it was boring."

"Well, it's a really big thing again in my time," I told him. "If you want to make a fortune, buy a load of skateboards in about 1999 and open a shop in the town centre. There, that's my financial tip for the future. Oh, yes, and mobile phones. Get into selling mobiles and you'll clean up – you'll be a millionaire. There's hardly a kid on the streets nowadays that hasn't got their own mobile. Teenage girls spend their entire lives sending each other stupid text messages."

"Text messages? What are they?" Welly was wide-eyed. The prospect of being a millionaire had clearly set those little cogs whirring.

"Look, Welly, I haven't come all this way just to tell you how to make your fortune. That's not my reason for being here."

I put my head in my hands and sighed with despair. Why, out of all the people in the entire bloody universe, was I stuck with *him*? Weird Welly was no way weird enough to cope with this. OK, he'd reacted with some amazement but no more than if I had told him that Southend-on-Sea were now Champions of Europe.

"Something wrong?" Welly asked me quietly, leaning forward into what must have looked like thin air.

It was pointless letting the guy annoy me. He was the only person who could see and hear me – apart from the little girl on the bus, and she wouldn't be any help.

"What is your reason, then?" he persisted. "What's 'The Mission'?"

"I'm not here to save the world, Welly. I'm not bloody Superman... It's just a personal thing ... unfinished business."

"Right..." said Welly, starting to grasp the significance of the situation. "So, this thing, it's to do with me?"

"Sort of."

"What happens to me? In the future – what happens?"

"Maybe I shouldn't tell you," I said.

"Is it bad, then?"

"No, it's not bad."

"But not good?"

"I can't say."

"Why not? Come on, you've got to!"

I shook my head. "No, no... I wouldn't have wanted to know. If someone had said that I was going to die when I was only sixteen, I probably wouldn't have believed them."

"But perhaps they could have stopped it happening."

"Yes, Welly," I replied pointedly. "Perhaps they could." I looked at his pale, blotchy face, spotty with youth. My memory added the lines round his mouth, the patches of hard stubble, the grey shadows beneath his eyes. Maybe it was the fluorescent light of the restaurant or maybe it was Welly's age, but the greenness of his eyes seemed deeper than I remembered – less watery, not as sad.

"What's your name?" he asked.

"I can't tell you yet."

"Why not? Are we related?"

"No. We're just friends," I replied carefully.

"Am I married? Have I got kids?"

"No, not that I know of. You might have been married once, but you never talked about it. I don't think you've got kids. But you might have – I don't know."

"You don't know much about me, do you? Are you sure we're mates?"

"Yes, yes … but, now I think about it, I didn't know you very well… I came into your shop looking for a drum kit … I'm a drummer – was a drummer," I corrected. "Wasn't much good. I was pretty crap, actually. But I'd only been playing for a few months."

"So I run a music shop, do I?"

"Yeah, something like that… I'm feeling tired, Welly. I need to think."

"And the band? What happens to Stride?"

"I don't know exactly. I need to think about it."

I rose from my seat and made for the door. I was confused, exhausted. I had come to find Welly, expecting wisdom, advice, guidance, answers. But he was nothing but a goon. He followed me out of the restaurant, tagging at my heels as I walked down the street. It was still raining, in long, thick sheets. Within seconds, Welly was soaking wet, but I remained as dry as a bone.

It was my street and yet not my street. Buses and cars were driving down the pedestrianized centre, and most of the shops were different – nothing was where I wanted it to be. I walked into an empty side road and rested against the wall. I felt dizzy and disorientated. Why couldn't I make myself invisible and get away from him?

"Tell me what happens," he demanded. "I've got to know now. They chuck me out of the band, is that it? It's Garry that does it, isn't it? Garry sacks me, just as we're about to hit it big. I knew it – I knew it! They only asked me to join because I had my own keyboard... Is Stride huge now? Is it one of those giant bands, like Roxy Music or the Rolling Stones? Are they all swanning it by some frigging swimming pool in the Caribbean while I'm stuck in some grotty music shop? Is that what happens? Tell me – you've got to tell me!"

"No, that's not what happens. Just leave me alone, will you? I'm tired. I've got to rest."

"They don't chuck me out, then?"

"No! I don't know – they might do... I don't know..."

"So what happens to the band?"

"Nothing!" I cried. "Nothing happens to the bloody band!"

I walked on, getting slower with every step. I had no energy left. It was easy for him to keep up.

"Why are you here?" he shouted at me. "I never asked you to come! I don't want to be haunted by some frigging ghost!"

I couldn't walk any more. I felt as if I was about to collapse. "Maybe we..." I grasped for the words but they spun out of reach. My head was reeling – the darkness was coming upon me again. "Maybe we can ... change ... things... But it's not ... you... It's – it's..."

"What?" he cried. "What?"

"It's Murph..." I gasped, falling away into nothingness. "We've got to save Murph."

13

When I next "woke up", I found myself in exactly the same place as when I had first arrived – sitting on the low front wall of the same unfamiliar house. Only this time, I understood why. This was Welly's house – I knew straightaway because he was in the garden, mowing the front lawn. I could tell by the slouch of his back. I watched him for a few moments, thinking to myself that there was no point in fighting the situation. Whoever was in charge of these matters had obviously decided that Welly was my destiny.

When he turned the mower round and saw me, he let go of the handle with a cry and the machine careered into the flower-bed. "Don't do that!" he shouted.

"Sorry, can't help it." Before I could say any more, Welly's mum opened the front-room window and screamed at him.

"Why can't you be careful, Pete? You've ruined my busy Lizzies!"

"Sorry, Mum," he called back, giving me a wary glance. But there was nothing to worry about. Welly's gift of seeing ghosts certainly hadn't been inherited from his mother. Mrs Llewellyn drew heavily on her cigarette and puffed an irritated smoke signal out of the window.

"You're not going to that practice until you've finished, you understand? And that includes bagging up the clippings!" She slammed the window shut. Welly sighed and turned to me.

"I thought you was just a nightmare," he said.

"I thought you *were*," I grinned. "What's the date?"

"I don't know … twenty-fourth or twenty-fifth. You've been gone a week."

"A whole week? Are you sure?"

I was stunned. Where had I been all that time? I had no idea. I realized that I could have been anywhere, done anything. Perhaps I had wandered off and caused havoc in the Middle Ages, or maybe I had zoomed into the Future – whatever I'd done, I had no memory of it.

"Yeah, it's been one of the worst weeks of my life, as a matter of fact," moaned Welly. "England got knocked out by Argentina on Sunday. And they cheated. Bloody Maradona, he wants shooting."

"Oh, it was *that* game, was it?" I said casually. "The famous Hand of God… Well, we got our revenge this summer – we beat Argentina."

"So you *do* know something about football." Welly gave me a reproving look.

"Not really. But nobody could avoid knowing about that game," I replied.

He came and sat next to me on the wall. "Why did you have to come back?"

"I've no control over it. I just keep turning up here. Sorry, but it looks like we're stuck with each other."

"Frigging great," muttered Welly. "Let's go inside. I don't want people to see me talking to myself."

"Aren't you supposed to bag up the clippings?"

"Nah, leave it till next time," he replied, scattering the grass over next door's overgrown flower-beds.

Welly took me up to his bedroom. It was very different from Murph's. His keyboard was tucked neatly down the side of his wardrobe and there wasn't a single band poster on the walls. It was like a younger boy's room, with blue-and-white striped wallpaper in his team's colours and a football duvet cover.

I sat on the bed while Welly told me that Murph, Garry and Shez had left school the year before and had been on the dole ever since. He was at college, the same college that I had gone to. Not that he appeared to be doing much there. There was a fine layer of dust on a shelf of textbooks, and various items of unused stationery were lined up on the desk.

"Can I?" he ventured, nervously reaching out to touch me on the shoulder. His hand stopped about a millimetre short. "It's like a force field," he said, shaking his fingers as if I'd just given him a mild electric shock. "All around your body... Weird."

"It's weird for me, too."

"Yeah, suppose it must be. My nan had a dog once," Welly replied.

"What's that got to do with anything?"

"She claimed it could see ghosts. Once, they took it on holiday to a cottage in Wales. It wouldn't even go in the place. Turned out the previous owner had died there just a few months before. Spooky, eh?"

"I think some children can see ghosts, too," I replied. "There was a little girl on the bus – she waved at me."

"No kidding? Was she scared?"

"Not at all..." There was a pause.

"What did you mean – we have to save Murph?" Welly asked cautiously, remembering my final words to him the week before.

"If I tell you, you must promise me you won't tell anyone else."

"Who could I tell? They'd think I was nuts. Probably shut me up in some loony bin."

I stood up and looked out of the window at the street below. Was I doing the right thing? "Murph is..." I hesitated.

"Is what?"

"He's about to die."

Welly stared down at his blue patterned carpet. "I thought you were going to say something like that," he said, his voice trembling. "How?"

"In a car crash."

Welly took a sharp intake of breath.

"Christ..."

"Sorry."

"And you're here because..." Welly frowned and shook his head. "Because you want me to save him? You want me to save his life?"

"Yes, I think so... I haven't a clue why I'm here, to tell you the truth. I'm not under any instructions from God ... or anyone else for that matter... I don't even know if it's possible to change things. I mean, it's already happened – well, in my time, it has – so maybe—"

"That's why the band splits up," interrupted Welly.

"Yes. If Murph doesn't die, it'll make a huge difference to everything," I admitted. "To all of us."

"Like how?"

"Well, maybe Stride will be a big success, and you'll all be rich and famous instead of..." I paused. "Well, let's just say I reckon things would be a lot better. Everyone would be a lot happier – like Murph's mum, for instance. She's never got over it. She's still in a really bad way."

"Well, Murph's all she's got. She worships him. Thinks he's perfect."

"Yes. I know her – well, knew her."

"So..." said Welly solemnly. "You'd better tell me... When does it happen?"

"That's the trouble," I sighed. "I can't remember the date exactly."

"What?" Welly leapt up from his chair and stared at me angrily. "How can I stop it if you won't tell me when it happens! Come on, you must know – you must!"

"Calm down!" I shouted back. "I haven't come here in a time machine, you know. I had no idea I was going to die – nobody warned me, Welly!" I stared accusingly at him. "I didn't make any plans or jot down dates on a piece of paper."

"I wish you bloody had," said Welly ruefully. He looked at his alarm clock and swore. "Practice! I daren't miss it again!" He took a large dollop of gel out of a tub and rubbed it into his hair.

◀◀ 136

"But we need to talk!"

"Then you'll have to come with me" – he dragged out his keyboard and tucked it under his arm – "meet the others."

We walked down the road in the direction of Murph's house. Welly was sweating with nerves, breathing heavily. He stared at all the passers-by, trying to work out if they could see me, but they looked right through my body ... although I couldn't help noticing that everyone gave him a few feet of space on his left side.

"You must have *some* idea when he's going to die," he hissed out of the side of his mouth.

"All I know is that it's soon," I said. "Probably very soon. Murph died about five months before I was born. I remember working that out from his gravestone. My birthday's in December. Which means it was July... It's some date in July."

"That's next week!"

Welly crossed the road and took a short cut through a patch of waste ground by a row of tatty garages. It was a route I didn't know. I was trying to work out whether the garages had been knocked down and what had been built in their place, when he stopped suddenly and turned to face me.

"So that means your mum is pregnant with you right now?"

"Suppose she must be..." I muttered evasively.

"Who is she? Do I know her?"

"Let's just concentrate on Murph," I replied, looking away.

Welly leant heavily on a garage door. What little brain he had was whirring away in his head. At last he was starting to think, but I didn't like the direction his thoughts were taking.

"You know all about us, don't you?" he said after a few moments' silence. "You know me; you know Murph's mum. That means you're connected with the band in some way. You must be."

"I'm not your son, if that's what you're thinking."

"It wasn't difficult to work that one out," Welly replied sharply. "More's the pity." He was studying me closely. "It's Shez, isn't it? Your mum is Shez."

"It doesn't matter."

"You look like her," he persisted. "You've got the same dark hair, same white skin."

I didn't reply.

"That must mean Garry's your dad."

"Afraid so..." I said finally. "They called me Liam. In memory of Murph."

"Figures..." Welly slid his back down the garage door and crouched in the gravel. "Shez hasn't said anything about being pregnant. God ... I wonder what Garry thinks... I bet he's furious."

"Probably."

"Do they get married?"

"Oh, yes, shortly after I was born. And I've got a kid sister."

"Garry and Shez... I never thought it would last..." mused Welly, throwing tiny stones in the dust.

"Well, they're hardly the world's happiest couple. Dad hasn't had a job in ages. He spends half his time in the pub and the other half shouting at us. We never got on. I don't suppose he'll be that bothered now I'm gone…"

"But Shez will be, won't she?"

"I expect so … hope so…"

A vivid picture suddenly sprang into my head – my funeral. I saw Mum sobbing as she followed the coffin, her hand tightly clutching Zoe's, as if she was never going to let her go. It was a bright sunny day, the grave-yard was bursting with flowers, most of them for me. There was quite a good turnout – I was impressed. My grandparents were walking slowly down the gravel path, one of my nans lifting a hankie to her nose. Daz and CJ were standing quietly at the back of the line – CJ was trying not to sniffle. Daz put his arm on his shoulder. Even Gemma and her parents had bothered to come. She looked more like the grieving widow than anyone – wearing a long, black velvet dress and holding a single trembling rose. I knew all along that she'd had a soft spot for me. I scanned the whole scene, but I couldn't see Dad anywhere. The picture vanished as quickly as it had appeared. Was it just a morbid fantasy or a true vision? Had my Present briefly collided with Welly's Past? I had no idea. I just felt drenched by a huge wave of sadness.

"This is really happening, isn't it?" said Welly, break-ing the heavy silence. "Murph is actually going to die… It could be in a few days' time. And I'm the only one in the world that knows about it… Jesus…" He stood up and banged his fist hard on the garage door. "Why did you have to pick me?" he shouted. "Why me?"

"I don't know! You're just psychic or something."

"I can't be the only one. I bet Shez and Garry will be able to see you – they're your bloody parents, after all."

"And what would I say? 'Hi, Mum and Dad, I'm the ghost of the baby you're pregnant with'?"

"No, you don't have to tell them that. Just … just … oh, I don't know. But you can't leave it all to me – it's not fair. Not without trying the others first."

"But what if Murph can see me? Surely that would be worse."

"No, it wouldn't," Welly barked. "It would be good. You could tell him the news yourself."

The band had already started playing by the time we reached the Murphys' house. Welly rang the bell and we waited anxiously for Mary to answer.

"If she can see me, will she know straightaway what I am?" I whispered.

"How the hell should I know?"

"Well, do I look like a ghost?"

"You're not see-through if that's what you mean… You look pretty normal to me… Why won't she answer the bloody door?" He kept his finger on the bell for several seconds.

"I'm coming, I'm coming!" called a voice. Mrs Murphy opened the front door, wiping her soapy hands on a tea towel. "Where have you been, Pete? I told them not to start until everyone had arrived, but they wouldn't listen."

It was clear that she couldn't see me. I felt relieved. The last time I had seen Mary Murphy had been from the other side of the road. It gave me a fresh shock to see her so close up. She was herself and yet not herself. Her eyes were brighter, her movements quicker. As she gently told Welly off for arriving late, her mouth couldn't resist forming an indulgent smile. The only thing that hadn't changed in the last sixteen years was the small gold crucifix she wore around her neck.

"Here goes," whispered Welly as he opened the bedroom door. "Best of luck."

The band was in mid-song. Shez waved as we walked in. Garry ignored him and carried on playing. Murph smiled and gestured at Welly in between drumbeats to close the door behind him.

I knew straightaway that I was utterly invisible to them. I hadn't caused so much as a cold draught – not even a shiver down the spine. Welly looked briefly at me, then back again at his fellow musicians. He looked downcast.

"Sorry," I said. "Looks like it's just me and you."

There they were – my mum and dad – themselves and yet not themselves. It was very, very strange. Mum was skinnier than ever, her dark hair spiked on top and cut sharply round her ears. Dad looked odd without his thinning hair and flabby stomach. His face was gaunt and a bit spotty. His legs looked like two thin black sticks. And behind the beautiful, gleaming drum kit was somebody who – according to my version of Time – was as dead as I was, if not deader. Murph was the only one who would never change – who would never grow older and fatter, never get the sack from a low-paid job, never hit his wife or swear at his children. Here was someone destined to die with his dreams intact, as

I supposed I had done. Not that it seemed much compensation now.

Welly fumbled with the zip of his keyboard case and tried to plug in as fast as he could.

"Where was you on Tuesday? It's not good enough. If you're late again, you're out, d'yer hear me?" shouted Garry the second he hit the last chord. Murph's final cymbal crash seemed to emphasize the threat.

Welly winced. "I couldn't help it, OK?"

"Something up?" asked Shez. "You all right?"

"Yes! Just get off my back, will you?" Welly twiddled some knobs and tried out a few jarring chords.

"Garry's got a point," reasoned Murph. "We haven't got long before the Battle of the Bands. We still can't play the new songs through properly."

"I know. I'm nearly ready."

"Well, nearly ready isn't good enough!" stormed Garry. "We'll never win unless idiot-features starts getting his arse here on time."

"Don't call me idiot-features, OK?"

"Oooh, I'm scared!" mocked Garry.

"Come on, let's play." Murph twirled his drumsticks expertly round his fingers.

"All I'm saying is, I don't want people in my band who won't take it seriously," insisted Garry.

"Since when has it been *your* band?" demanded Murph.

"All right, our band – the band. Last year we came second without a keyboard player; this year we can win without one."

"But everybody's using keyboards these days. All the songs are worked out. Come on, Garry," soothed Shez. "Let's just play."

"You don't understand – nobody understands! I want us to really go somewhere. I want Stride to be big! And this joker is holding us back!"

Welly let out a hollow laugh.

"That amuses you, does it?" snarled Garry.

"Yeah, it does, actually," Welly scoffed.

"Don't say anything, Welly!" I shouted from the corner.

Welly glanced over to me but didn't reply. He had knowledge, and knowledge was power.

"When Stride splits up, it won't be because of me," he said slowly.

"No, Welly," I urged.

"Who said anything about splitting up?" asked Murph.

"Do you want to be in this band or not?" asked Garry. "'Cos I don't get your attitude."

"Can we just get on?" shouted Shez.

"You can be a loser for the rest of your life if you want, Welly," Garry continued. "But I'm going to do something."

"No you're not," insisted Welly. "You're the loser, not me. At least I end up with my own shop. You end up on the dole. Can't even support your own kids."

"Welly! Stop it!" I cried.

At the same time, Garry shouted, "What the hell are you going on about?"

"I know what happens to all of us."

I rushed forward. I was standing right in front of Welly, but he scarcely blinked. "Don't say another word!" I threatened. But Welly didn't want to listen.

"You can't treat me like this," he went on, "because I know the truth. I've been – been … visited! I've been told about the future. I know what's going to happen to all of us."

"I know what's going to happen to you in a minute," shouted Garry. "You're going to get my fist in your face."

If I could have punched Welly, I would have done it myself.

"I know all about Shez for a start," he carried on defiantly.

"Oh yeah? And what's that?" Garry taunted. "Come on, get out your crystal ball, Welly. Spill the beans."

"No, Welly! Don't you dare!" I screamed.

"I'm not saying. But I know, that's all." Welly shot Shez a pointed look.

"Look, just forget it, will you? This is stupid!" interrupted Shez.

"She's right. It's a waste of time," added Murph. "We'll do the gig on Saturday and then we can talk about what happens next. Let's just play."

"What's the bloody point?" Welly collapsed on the bed, his head in his hands. "It all goes wrong – all of it! The band splits up – we do nothing with our lives. Nothing! I've been told – I've been visited."

"Welly, what are you talking about?"

"Nobody else can see him, only me."

"Are you on the glue again?"

Murph got off his stool and sat next to Welly.

"Who's visited you?"

"The police?" offered Shez helpfully. "Social worker? Someone from college?"

"No! Him! He's here now!" Welly screamed. "I can see him and hear him. He's standing right there! Look!" Welly burst into tears. His whole body was shaking as he pointed a trembling finger in my direction.

"There's nothing there, Welly," said Shez, sitting on his other side. She glanced at Murph worriedly. "Perhaps you should get your mum to take a look at him."

"Nah ... he's on something, that's all. What you bin taking, Welly?" demanded Garry. "And why didn't you let us have some of it?" He laughed cruelly at his own joke.

"Look, there ... look hard! He's standing right there! About our age, baggy jeans, black hair..."

"They can't see me, Welly," I said. "Don't say any more, please..."

"It's your fault!" he screamed at me. "Why did you have to tell me the future?"

"Because I want to change it. For all our sakes."

"How can we change it? It's already happened."

"Jesus!" muttered Garry. He twisted his finger next to his head in a mocking gesture of insanity. "Now he's hearing voices."

"I knew they wouldn't believe me," sobbed Welly.

"Then why did you have to blurt it all out?" I answered, standing over him, trembling with anger. Shez was stroking his back, telling him to calm down.

She looked straight at me, and I suddenly longed for her to be able to see me. I had missed her so much.

A black sleep was starting to take over my senses. I felt overcome with tiredness, my limbs were growing heavy; I couldn't move. I was fading again... A few more minutes, and I would be gone.

"Welly, stop it," said Shez. "There's nothing to worry about. Honest."

"You've got a secret, haven't you, Shez?" Welly grabbed her hand in desperation. "See, I know what it is. Liam told me."

"I never said anything!" Murph interrupted.

"Not you," said Welly weakly. "The other Liam."

"I think we should call the men in white coats," declared Garry.

"Stop it, Garry, he's not well!" shouted Shez. "Can't you see that? Feel his head – he's burning up." She laid Welly gently back on the bed and peeled the sticky, gelled hair away from his forehead.

"I'm all right," he murmured, turning away. "He's fading... He's going now..."

I don't know exactly what happened next because I disappeared.

14

"I'm out of the band now and it's your fault!" cried Welly. I had "popped up out of nowhere" at the bus stop just round the corner from his house. Not quite such an accurate landing this time but near enough for us to bump into each other within an hour or so of my arrival. It was a warm, sticky day, late afternoon or early evening – I couldn't tell exactly.

"You've only yourself to blame," I answered back. "Why did you have to go blabbing to everyone?"

"Your bloody father made me angry, that's why." Welly grimaced and lit a cigarette. "God, I thought my parents were awful, but at least I don't have to put up with someone like him."

"Tell me about it!" I replied.

"Anyway, I didn't say anything about Murph, or that Shez was pregnant."

"You came pretty near."

"Yeah, well, I didn't, OK? After you vanished into thin air Murph and Garry took me home. Told my parents I was having a nervous breakdown. Just what I need."

"And they chucked you out of the band?"

"On health grounds – would you believe it? That's what Garry said. He was just looking for an excuse. He's been wanting me out for ages."

"Why?"

"'Cos he's a git." He took a long drag and blew smoke into the sky. I watched it drift upwards and then disintegrate into the atmosphere.

"How long have I been gone?" I asked.

"Not long enough!" he growled.

"Tell me – how long?"

"A few days… It's July now… Frigging Argentina won the whole bloody thing, you know. Makes me sick. The only good thing about it was they beat Germany." He threw his fag onto the pavement and stamped the glowing stub into the ground.

The number 65 arrived and Welly got on. It wasn't possible to talk on the bus, so we sat in silence. I was cross with Welly. Now he was out of Stride, it was going to be harder for him to do anything about Murph. He only had a ghost of a chance in the first place. The phrase made me chuckle grimly to myself. Now I knew from experience it meant no chance at all.

The bus ride down the hill and into the town centre gave me time to think. There were probably only a few people who could see me, and I didn't seem to have any powers at all. I couldn't move the smallest piece of furniture or make the curtains blow mysteriously or scatter papers across a desk. I couldn't appear and disappear at will or travel vast distances with a click of my fingers. I might as well have been watching the Past on a giant television screen. My only chance of influencing events was through Welly. Welly! Why couldn't I have been given somebody with more than half a brain to help me change history? It made me want to chuck it all in and go home – except I didn't know whether I even had a home in the spirit world, let alone how to get there.

"So how are we going to save Murph now?" I asked once we were walking down a quiet side road off the High Street. Welly was striding along, his lips pursed and his heavy eyebrows locked in an irritable frown. I had to run to keep up.

"What's it got to do with me? Why should I care whether Stride turns out to be big?" He crossed the road and headed towards Stillwells, a large music shop on the corner. "Serves them all right if they do split up."

"But you can't say that. We're talking about somebody's life here!"

Welly shrugged as he pushed open the door. He made for the keyboards department and spent about twenty minutes drooling over the latest Yamahas. They all seemed pretty basic to me – in fact, they made Daz's tatty old keyboard look space-age by comparison. Welly chatted cheerfully to the assistant about the various "amazing" new features and cracked a few dreadful jokes. He was behaving completely normally, as if he hung around with ghosts from the Future every day of the week. I tried my best to put him off by shouting in his face and jumping around in his path, but he simply ignored me.

The next stop was the noticeboard on the landing between the guitar and drums department. This was where bands advertised for new members.

Welly scanned the tatty bits of paper scrawled in felt pen with lots of urgent underlinings. *Excellent keyboard player wanted immediately – loads of gigs lined up, signing imminent!* or *Futuristic band seek brilliant keyboard player. Must have own transport.*

"Any of these names mean anything to you?" he whispered.

I hadn't heard of any of them, although I was no expert in Eighties music. Maybe one of these bands ended up with a single in the top forty – I didn't know. But Welly's question gave me an idea.

"Now, that would be telling, wouldn't it?" I said as mysteriously as I could.

His eyes lit up. "What do you mean? Who? Who makes it big? Expanding Heads? Streamline? The Liberators? Which one?"

"I'm not saying unless you help me."

"Come on, you know there's nothing I can do about Murph. You can't change what's already happened."

"In which case, there's no point in you trying to join one of those bands," I replied. "Pity… You could have had an amazing future." I had him well and truly hooked. Welly tore a poster off the wall and borrowed a pencil from a guy in guitars. He frantically scribbled down the details for every single advert – even the ones asking for guitarists and drummers. It was hard not to laugh at him, he looked so desperate, but I had to keep playing it cool.

"If Murph's still alive by the end of July, I'll tell you which band to go for," I declared.

"But they might have found somebody else by then!"

"So you'll have to apply to be in every single one."

"This isn't fair, what you're doing! It's torture!" he wailed.

"I'd keep your voice down if I were you. People are looking."

We walked out of the shop and back to the bus stop in stony silence. At last I felt I had some power. Welly had a grim expression on his face, as if he had just made a pact with the Devil.

The bus was pretty crowded on the way back to Corsfield. It was end-of-school time and we had to stand. I didn't mind – it gave me the opportunity to put my plan to Welly in a place where he couldn't run away or answer back.

"First I want you to go and see Shez. Don't mention that you've been visited again – it sounds ridiculous. And steer clear of the ghost stuff. Just say you've been having dreams or premonitions or something. You've discovered you've got psychic powers. Say it's in the family. Don't tell her the story about your nan's dog – pets don't count. Keep it simple, matter-of-fact. Whatever you do, don't go all hysterical on her again. Tell her what you know about Murph. If she doesn't believe you, you'll have to tell her that you know she's pregnant. Say she's expecting a son who's going to be born on December twelfth. Obviously, she'll know you're telling the truth about that, which makes it more likely that she'll believe the stuff about Murph. I think she'd have a much better chance of saving him than you – now you've managed to get yourself chucked out of Stride, anyway."

Welly nodded, but he didn't look happy about it.

We got off three stops before Welly's house and made our way to Shez's place. It was a shock when I realized it was the same house that my grandparents still lived in – a small terrace with the same blue front door. Shez was surprised to see Welly standing on the step.

"Is Garry with you?" was his first question.

"No, sorry. You'll find him with Murph."

"Actually, it's you I want to talk to."

Shez let out a long, bored sigh, as if she knew what was coming next.

"It's Garry and Murph's band, you know, not mine. If they won't have you back there's nothing I can do about it."

"I wouldn't come back to Stride if you paid me," Welly assured her – somewhat foolishly I thought – as Shez led him into the living room. "I'm joining another band. A better band."

"Oh yeah, what's that?"

"I can't say yet. Confidential."

Shez sat on the sofa and kicked her legs up. Her tiny feet were bare and she had painted her toenails purple. The sight of them made me feel dizzy with memory – it was something Mum still did. I remembered her sitting with her feet on the cushions, painting her toenails one by one: sometimes red, sometimes pink, even glittery silver at Christmas. It used to puzzle me, this weekly ritual – particularly as she never went anywhere to show them off. Most of the year her toes were hidden under her socks.

"Well, if you don't want to come back to the band, what do you want?" Shez sighed.

Welly perched on the edge of an armchair and coughed. "I, er, wanted to apologize for that scene the other day. I wasn't feeling well and, er, I said a few stupid things."

"Well, I wouldn't worry. Nobody understood what you were going on about."

"It's just that…" Welly took a deep breath. "I've discovered that I'm psycho."

"Psychic," I interrupted.

"I mean psychic… It's a family thing. Some of us have it, some don't."

"OK," replied Shez. "And?"

"I've discovered that I can see into the future."

Shez suppressed a giggle.

"No, it's true, I can. I have these, er … these things beginning with p … like dreams … um…"

"Premonitions," I prompted irritably. "Get on with it, Welly, or she'll fall asleep on you."

Shez was yawning and fiddling with a silver chain around her neck.

"Yes, premonitions… I know that in a few weeks' time, maybe a few days, Murph is going to die."

Shez sat bolt upright.

"I didn't mean that quickly, idiot!" I shouted.

Welly shot me an angry glance.

"Don't say that sort of thing, Welly, it's not funny."

Shez paced over to the window and stared angrily down the garden. I could see my grandad's vegetable patch – the same neat rows of lettuces and beetroot, carrots and runner beans that he still grew every year.

"It's true. He dies in a car accident ... sometime soon..."

"You're sick, do you know that? You can't bear it that they chucked you out the band so now you're going to make trouble." She was steaming with anger. "I think you'd better go," she said coldly.

"And the other thing I know is..." Welly paused for effect. "You're pregnant."

"How dare you!" Shez turned on him immediately. "You better not have said that to anyone else 'cos it's not true."

"But it is," protested Welly. He looked at me and I shrugged. Shez was blushing, but her gaze was steady. "You're going to have a boy," he continued. "He's born on, er ... December something ... yes, December twelfth."

"Garry's right – you're completely off your head."

"But I know it's true!" Welly insisted.

"Please just get out and leave me alone!" she cried.

"Do one of those tests, then. Go on, I dare you, do a pregnancy test. You'll see I'm right."

"I don't need to do a test! I know I'm not pregnant. Now get out!" Shez almost chased Welly out of the door and slammed it on his back. She was so quick I didn't have time to sneak out behind him. I watched him through the window. He hung around in the front garden for a few moments, looking vaguely up at the roof as if I was going to waft out of the chimney. Once he'd realized I was stuck inside he wandered off, his hands in his pockets. No doubt he was now off to join every no-hope band in town, in the hope that I was going to reveal which one was the next Duran Duran.

Shez leant heavily on the front door and bit her lip. Tears were welling up in her dark eyes – she looked unsteady on her feet. Welly had rattled her, for sure. But she wasn't going to let on to him that she was pregnant. My mum was never that daft. I was impressed by her performance – she'd played it really cool. After checking that Welly was well and truly out of sight, she dragged on a pair of white shoes and a silky blue bomber jacket. Then she stuck a small leather purse in her pocket and left the house. I followed. I didn't like creeping around after my mother like this, but I had to do something. Welly didn't seem able to follow the simplest instructions without mucking them up.

I followed Shez to the parade of local shops. I knew these shops well – or rather, I knew the future versions of them well. This was where my nan and grandad had sent me to buy their *News of the World* on a Sunday morning when I had been sent to stay with them for the weekend. That was several years ago, when Mum and Dad used to go out together on Saturdays, before Zoe was born and Dad lost his job. The newsagent was in the same place, just with a different sign on the front. I had guessed that Shez was going to buy fags to calm her nerves, but she walked straight past and into the chemist that was destined to become a Chinese takeaway.

"Pregnancy test," I muttered to myself. "She's gone to get a pregnancy test." I was right. Back we went to my grandparents' house. Shez was walking quickly, clipping along in her high-heeled shoes as if she was late for something. I guessed she wanted to do the dreaded deed before my nan got home from work. It wasn't easy to keep up with her, but I had to stay close to be sure of getting back inside the house. If only she knew, I thought to myself, if only she knew that I was right behind her. She was my mum and yet not my mum. Here and now she was just a fragile teenage girl. It was strange to think that she had been the one I had turned to when things had gone wrong – a scrap in the play-ground, getting suspended from school for not wearing proper uniform, my GCSE results, to name but a few. I had never questioned her fitness for the job. She was my mum and I could rely on her, just as in the last few years she had come to rely on me. Many times I'd come home from school and seen that her face was blotchy with crying. We'd have a cup of tea and watch chil-dren's TV huddled up on the sofa together. Half an hour of blaring American cartoons seemed to soothe her. She'd drag herself up, ruffle my hair and pad off to the kitchen to make the dinner. There was no need to talk about her problems – we both knew the cause... But I wasn't there for her any more. She was alone. I was pretty sure Mum would be missing me by now.

Shez let herself back in the house and rushed up the stairs to the bathroom. I was hit by an overwhelming sense of dread. Her dread, I suppose. She didn't want the test to be positive. She didn't want to be pregnant.

When the little indicator thing turned pink or blue or whatever it did, it would signal the start of a downhill slide. Suddenly I knew that it wasn't just Murph's death that had caused everything to go wrong: it was me.

I stayed outside the bathroom door, so I did not witness the actual moment of discovery. I just sat on the top stair and wished that ghosts could cry. After a few moments Shez emerged. Her face had that familiar blotchy look – her eyes were liquid. She was devastated … and I could do nothing to comfort her. I couldn't even hold her hand.

15

I was desperate to get out of the house, but Shez didn't seem to want to go anywhere. She ran into her bedroom and shut the door firmly behind her. I had no choice but to go downstairs and wait for the door to open so that I could slip out. It was early evening. With a bit of luck my grandparents would soon be back from work.

I wandered round the room, two rooms, in fact, which had been knocked into one. It felt very familiar. They had the same wallpaper – large grey-green leaves on a straw-coloured background – and the same moss-green carpet, although of course it looked newer than I remembered. My grandparents' collection of family photos was even sitting in the same place on the wooden shelving unit in the alcove. All that was missing was pictures of me.

Grandad turned up first, letting himself in by the back door, so that I missed his arrival. He poured himself a beer and switched on the telly. I sat in the other armchair and studied his features – his hair was thicker, the colour of his eyes more solid, his chin less flabby. He looked at ease with himself. If the rest of his life were to be filled with Friday nights down the British Legion and the annual fortnight in Skeggie, he wasn't going to complain. Grandad's plans for the future probably never stretched beyond a small extension to the kitchen. He didn't need to look ahead because he was expecting to have more of the same. Only I knew that he was going to be made redundant at the awkward age of fifty-nine and nearly have a nervous breakdown; that he would spend the rest of his days sitting by the side of the canal with a fishing rod limply in his hand; that he would grow bitter and ashamed, while Nan would take on a new lease of life as a much-loved dinner lady. I was so busy feeling sorry for my grandad that I missed Nan's entrance altogether.

"Tea's here!" she shouted, slamming the front door behind her. "Hurry up before it gets cold." She scurried into the kitchen and unwrapped three portions of fish and chips.

"Ian, get the knives and forks out, will you? Do something!"

"Give us a chance, duck," he called back.

"Is Sheryl in?"

"She should be."

"Give her a call, then!"

After Grandad had nearly shouted himself hoarse, Shez emerged from her room and dragged her feet down the stairs. If she had been crying she had done an expert job of disguising the fact with make-up. The three of them ate in virtual silence with the plates on their laps. Once the news ended, Grandad flicked from channel to channel, the remote control in one hand and his greasy fork in the other.

"There's never anything on of a Thursday," he complained.

"Stop doing that, will you?" retorted Nan. "You'm giving me a headache."

It was odd watching them shovel the food into their mouths with the occasional mumble to pass the tomato sauce. Nan was already well on the way to becoming that large jolly woman that five-year-olds loved to hug in the playground. I couldn't work out whom Shez had inherited her boniness from. Not that she was going to look slim for much longer. A few times I saw her hand lingering thoughtfully on her tummy, but apart from that she betrayed nothing of her newly discovered state. I wondered when she was going to tell them. Not in front of *The Two Ronnies*, that was for sure.

After tea, Shez made some excuse for going back to her room – I decided not to follow her; it didn't seem right. So I remained in the lounge while my grandparents proceeded to argue over what to watch on the box. For the first time in my existence as a ghost, I felt bored. I longed for my grandad to nip down to the pub or for my nan to pop out to post a letter – anything to get them to open the front door so that I could escape. I even wished I could fade away for one of my strange spells in Dark Oblivion. Anything would be better than watching ancient quiz shows and unfunny sitcoms.

I wandered around the house for a short while, not that there was much to see in the bedrooms or bathroom.

Nan was a great one for keeping doors shut and switching lights off, so I kept getting stuck in the hallway. At half past ten they went up to bed, leaving me to spend the night on the stairs. What was I supposed to do now? I couldn't sleep or make myself a snack or switch on the telly. All I could do was sit and wait for somebody to get up and open the bloody door.

I had stayed up all night before with Daz and CJ, drinking cheap lager and watching horror videos. That had been boring enough, but this was the limit. I listened to the constant hum of cars thundering down the motorway a few miles off. I eavesdropped on a tedious argument between two men in the street and heard a couple of cats scrapping in the garden.

Eventually dawn broke through the frosted glass on the front door and formed a rectangle of light on the hall carpet. At half past six, the milkman's van trundled up the street. A little later, a dark shadow shoved a small brown envelope through the letterbox. Eventually the clock in the hallway edged its way towards seven o'clock. I felt like a dog that had been shut up all night and was desperate to pee in the garden. "Come on!" I shouted at their closed bedrooms. "Get up, will you! Let me out!"

Ten minutes later, an alarm clock went off and a groggy-looking Grandad emerged from the bedroom. He padded downstairs to switch on the kettle, then went to the bathroom for a wash and shave. He took absolutely ages, while Nan hovered on the landing, knocking several times on Shez's door and telling her to "shift herself". I followed the three of them round as they gradually made it to breakfast, trying to guess who would open the front door first. It wasn't an easy job. Nan shut me in the kitchen while she brought in the milk, and then I managed to get stuck in the sitting room when Grandad left for work. Shez made a grudging appearance just as my nan was putting away the breakfast things.

"You'm going down the Job Centre today?" Nan asked. "You promised you would."

"Why do you think I got up so early?" snapped Shez as she retrieved the packet of Frosties from the cupboard.

"Call this early? It's gone nine. And wear something decent, in case you get an interview."

"I'm fine as I am."

"So you think."

Shez poured the milk. There were so few flakes of Frosties in her bowl I could count them. She ate listlessly, barely looking up from the table, as if scared to meet Nan's eyes.

"You all right, love?" Nan's tone was relenting. "You'm looking a bit peeky."

"There's nothing wrong with me, OK? I'm just tired."

"You're always tired these days. You don't eat enough."

"Just get off my back, will you?" snarled Shez. She pushed her chair back with an irritable screech and went back upstairs to finish getting ready. Her teenage behaviour would have amused me if I hadn't known how much she was suffering inside.

I finally got out of the house at half past nine. I had planned to find Welly and tell him that Shez was definitely pregnant, but now I wasn't convinced that it was such a good move. The poor girl had enough problems without that fool hanging around her. So I decided to stick with "Mum". She turned the corner and crossed the road, making her way past Murph's house and through the short cut by the garages. When she reached St Cedd's Church, she took the main road but away from the direction of the town centre. If the Job Centre hadn't moved in the last sixteen years, she definitely wasn't going there. Perhaps this was the way to Garry's house. I kept pace with her, silent, invisible – beginning to fancy myself as her guardian angel. I wondered whether Shez sensed me in any way, whether she would tell Garry that she had felt she was being followed or that somebody was watching her. But it wasn't Garry she was going to see. It was the doctor.

"You should have made an appointment," said the receptionist with a frown. She had tightly permed hair and enormous glasses.

"I didn't have time. It's an emergency," Shez insisted.

The receptionist briefly looked her up and down, as if searching for something that required urgent medical attention – a bandaged hand, a swollen ankle, a sore red nose. Then she saw the tragic look in Shez's eyes. "OK," she said reluctantly. "I'll try and squeeze you in."

Forty-five minutes later and we were in the doctor's consulting room. I knew I shouldn't have gone in there with her, but I wanted to know what she was going to say.

"Oh, you girls," Dr Barker sighed when Shez told him she was pregnant. "What are we going to do with you?"

"I want an abortion," she replied without hesitation.

I felt my knees give way from under me. This wasn't right, couldn't be right.

"Have you discussed it with the father?" Dr Barker sat back in her revolving chair and put down her pen.

"No. I don't want him to know." Shez's tone was sharp and businesslike. Her eyes were dry, her hands steady.

"But surely you should at least talk it over with him?"

"No. I've already decided; there's no way I want this baby. It's my body, so it's my decision."

"Let's see how far gone you are, then," sighed Dr Barker.

She took Shez into a separate room to examine her. I sat on the doctor's desk, Shez's hard, cold words reverberating in my head. She felt none of that teenage maternal pull I had seen among a few of the girls at college. She had no desire to ooh and aah at baby clothes – no longing to push a living doll around in a pram. She couldn't have made her position any clearer. There wasn't so much as a chink of hope. My mum didn't want me – had probably never wanted me. She didn't intend for me to be born.

"You're about four months pregnant," Dr Barker said as they re-entered the consulting room. "Another couple of weeks, and it would have been too late to arrange a termination. Why did you leave it so long before coming to see me?"

"I was trying to ignore it."

Dr Barker raised her eyebrows.

"I know – it was stupid … but we only did it once. I thought it couldn't happen the first time…"

"Lots of girls get caught out that way," said Dr Barker. "Surely you noticed yourself putting on a bit of weight?"

Shez shook her head.

"Haven't you been feeling sick or anything?"

"Yes, a bit, but I have a weak stomach anyway."

"So what made you decide to come and see me?"

"Well, it sounds ridiculous, but this lad, he's a sort of friend I suppose, he told me he'd seen into the future. He said I was going to have a son on December twelfth."

"You can't be serious."

"He did, honest. It really gave me the creeps. So I thought I'd better do a test and find out for sure."

"December twelfth… How extraordinary." The doctor ran her finger across a calendar on the desk. "I'd put your due date down as December seventh."

"So he was wrong then?"

"Not necessarily. Hardly any babies arrive on the day you expect them. About one in a hundred, I believe… How very strange."

"Well, he has got it wrong because I'm getting rid of it," said Shez defiantly. "As soon as possible."

Dr Barker filled out a form and wrote a brief letter. It was all so quick and simple. I couldn't understand why she didn't try to persuade Shez to keep me. Why didn't she insist that Shez's parents were informed or that Shez talked to Garry? Couldn't she arrange some kind of counselling? Surely they had counselling in the 1980s. It was all too much for me, too hurtful, too confusing. To think I had seen myself as my mum's guardian angel when all the time she was preparing to make sure I never existed!

I was too shaken to keep up with Shez after she left the doctor. I didn't know what her plans were for the rest of the day, and I didn't want to find out. I walked back to Welly's house and hung around, hoping he might turn up. In fact, he was lying in bed the whole time. He finally spotted me when he drew back his curtains and yawned vacantly out of the window.

"Oi, Welly!" I shouted. "Let me in!" I could see him hesitating – he nearly closed the curtains again. "I need to talk to you – it's really important!"

"I was hoping I'd seen the last of you," he muttered as he opened the front door a few minutes later. "Where did you get to last night?"

"Got stuck in Shez's house… Listen, Welly, I need your help. Something terrible is about to happen, and you've got to stop it."

"Don't tell me somebody else is about to die," he scoffed.

"Yes, they are, as a matter of fact. Me!"

"I thought you were already dead."

"If we don't do something, I'll never have existed at all."

"What the hell are you talking about now?" Welly took a pint of milk from the fridge and poured himself a glass. "I can't take much more of this. It's doing my head in. I haven't slept properly for days."

"Shez did a pregnancy test yesterday, after you left."

"And?"

"It was positive, of course. This morning she marched down to the doctor's and said she wanted an abortion!"

Welly whistled.

"Can't you see you've already changed the future?"

"It's not my fault!" retorted Welly. "I wouldn't worry too much. She'll probably change her mind tomorrow – decide she wants you after all. Girls do that sort of thing."

"No, no, she's really sure – it's being arranged. The doc said that if she had left it much longer it would have been too late. Then Shez told her that it was you that made her decide to do the pregnancy test!"

"She must have already known she was pregnant."

"She told the doc she wasn't sure. Said she was trying to ignore the problem, hoping it would solve itself, I suppose."

Suddenly the penny dropped. Welly's eyes widened and he put down his piece of freshly made toast and peanut butter. "So what happened before – in your Time I mean – is that Shez didn't know she was in the club until it was too late to do anything about it."

"Exactly. So she had to keep me and marry Garry."

"God … we really have put a spanner in the works," he muttered.

"Unless we find a way to stop Shez having the abortion."

"As well as preventing Murph from dying in a car

crash?" Welly laughed grimly. "Have you got any more disasters you'd like me to deal with? Earthquakes? Volcanic eruptions? World War Three?"

"You don't have to be sarcastic about it. This is my life we're talking about. I know it wasn't a great existence and it only lasted for sixteen years, but it's got to be better than nothing."

"Sorry, Liam. I can't help you... Even if I wanted to." Welly submerged his plate and glass in a bowl of cold soapy water and dried his hands on a tea towel. "They wouldn't listen to me."

"But now Shez knows you were telling the truth about the pregnancy, don't you think she might?"

He shrugged.

"You've got to go and see her again!" I urged. "Tell her she mustn't have the abortion."

"Perhaps I should tell her she *must* have it; then she'll keep you to spite me."

"I don't care how you do it – just try!"

Welly shook his head. "I'm sorry," he mumbled. "I can't. Please go away..."

16

I left Welly's house and wandered through the streets. Suddenly I had nowhere to go and nothing to do. Welly had let me down, and it wasn't the first time. Or maybe it was the first time, because this was happening before I was born. I couldn't make sense of it. If I really had just changed history, it meant that Mum was going to have an abortion. But then I would never have existed, which was impossible. Or was it? I reminded myself that I'd always thought travelling back in time was impossible; that ghosts were impossible. All my notions of possibility had been shot to pieces.

I had already lived my life, a rather short and fairly pointless one it had to be admitted – but there were documents with my name on it, photographs, dental records, clothes, shoes, personal possessions. Then there were my family and my friends, people at school, at college, the skaters on the library steps. They'd all have memories of me. I tried to imagine the last sixteen years in the life of the planet without the presence of Liam Condie. Would the world have been any different?

Of course not. But it would have made a huge difference to my mother.

I loved my mum, and I knew she loved me. Of course she was upset when she discovered she was pregnant, but I don't think she ever regretted having me. We'd always got on together pretty well. Perhaps she'd originally planned to have an abortion but changed her mind after Murph died. Yes, that made sense. But could I simply sit back and watch events play themselves out? Surely it was too much to risk. And what if her change of heart depended on Murph dying – did I have to let that happen, too?

I wished to God – and for once this plea was possibly being made in the right direction – that I hadn't just been dumped here without any preparation or training. Even my poxy sixth-form college gave us a whole day's induction course. They showed us around, vaguely mentioned a few rules, took our photos for the files and told us which curry houses would give student discounts. But no, we spirits were left to fend for ourselves, without so much as an introductory welcome speech or a copy of the *Spook Handbook*. I could think of loads of "Frequently Asked Questions" to put in such a publication. Like, where can I find a psychic person with more than half a brain? How can I learn to materialize or at least write an important message? And finally – are there any courses in How to Change the Course of History Without Accidentally Obliterating Your Own Existence?

I kept thinking about that *Superman* film where Lois Lane was killed. Superman flew into space and turned the planet with his bare hands until the whole universe went back in time. Then he zoomed back down to earth, plucked Lois to safety and nobody was any the wiser. But that had only been for a few minutes and, more to the point, it was a Hollywood movie. I needed to make sure Shez didn't go through with the abortion, and I wanted Murph to live, too. I just didn't know how to bring it about.

Welly was my only hope. Over the next few days I tried my best to cajole, bribe and threaten him into action, but nothing worked. Even the lure of joining a soon-to-be-famous band didn't motivate him. "It's not my fault" and "Sorry, I can't help you" turned into "You're just a figment of my imagination". Whenever I tried to talk to him, he covered his ears and fled, like a child being bullied in the playground. Welly decided that he was having a nervous breakdown – his visions of me were symptoms of his illness, rather than the cause. But I was persistent. I made faces at his living-room window while he was trying to eat his dinner; jumped out at him from behind the dustbins as soon as he tried to leave the house. I even stood in his front garden and screamed his name through the night. In the end, he stuffed his ears with his mother's make-up remover pads, locked himself in his bedroom, shut the windows and drew the curtains.

After three days his mum called the doctor round, who prescribed anti-depressants and referred them both to family therapy. It made me wonder how many other ghosts were wandering around, making psychically gifted teenagers believe they had gone completely mad.

So I had no choice but to turn my attentions to Shez. Of course I still wanted to save Murph, but I had to confess that the problem of my potential non-existence was taking over. I didn't know exactly when the abortion was booked for, but I suspected it was soon. I started to hang around outside Shez's house, sometimes all night long, half expecting her to climb out of her window with an overnight bag and shin down the drainpipe.

I became quite used to sharing the garden with the neighbourhood cats. One in particular, a small tabby with a pretty face and three white paws, seemed to know I was there. She sat next to me all night, purring and staring at me with unblinking, glowing eyes. I imagined she was a witch's cat who belonged to some crazy old woman mumbling over a cauldron in Rough Wood. I would give the witch all sorts of useful information about the future (if I could remember any, that is), and in return she would go and talk to Shez. But the cat left promptly as the dawn broke, leaping over the garden fence and disappearing through a cat-flap in next door's kitchen.

Shez was still intending to get rid of me – that much was certain. She had another appointment at the doctor's, then she visited the abortion clinic on the posh side of town, near where Gemma lived. One morning, I followed her down some leafy side road and into a large Victorian house. There was no sign that this was a private clinic, apart from blinds at the windows and several expensive cars in the sweeping gravel driveway. It was a bright, warm day, but the mood in the waiting room was decidedly grim. A few teenage girls were sitting in silence with their mothers, the girls' faces heavy with self-pity – their mothers tight-lipped and resentful. Shez walked in and plonked herself next to the window. She picked up a magazine and flicked idly through its pages, looking less nervous than as if she were waiting to see the dentist. I couldn't believe her indifference, her defiant casualness. She felt like a stranger to me.

I wandered out into the hallway and studied the posters on the noticeboard, most of them about various methods of contraception – crossing your fingers behind your back not being one of them. "Bit bloody late for all that," remarked a bitter mother as she led her defeated child into the consulting room. Then three girls bounced down the stairs, swinging small overnight bags. Their faces were tired and puffy but – it had to be admitted – shining with elation. Their nightmare was over. They were behaving like pupils from a boarding school going home for the holidays, all thanks and smiles, saying fond farewells to their chums – fellow patients they had probably only met a few hours before. I couldn't bear it a moment longer. I didn't go into the consulting room with Shez but slipped out with one of the happy, unpregnant ones and caught the bus back to Corsfield. I felt desperate, overwhelmed with rejection. There was nothing I could do. I would have to put my trust in history.

It was the middle of July now. Stride was practising virtually every day in Murph's bedroom. I always turned up with Shez and sat in the corner, watching them play. The room was thick with secrets. Outside, the weather was dry and hot, but the band still had to play with all the windows shut. Garry and Murph took off their T-shirts and let the sweat evaporate into the stale air. Every so often Garry went to the bathroom, returning with his head dripping with cold water. His body was pale and thin. Murph's back was covered in freckles and Garry had the delicate beginnings of a hairy chest. Shez kept complaining that they stank.

"Can't you at least use deodorant or something?" she moaned. She was feeling particularly sensitive to unpleasant smells. Shez was fighting to keep going as if nothing was wrong and, for the most part, she was winning. The only signs of her "condition" were her frequent trips to the toilet, wearing her tops over her jeans to hide her very slight bump, and throwing up one sweaty afternoon when Garry ate a packet of cheese and onion crisps.

With Welly's departure, all their songs had to be reworked. It turned out that Shez could play a bit of bass, so she and Garry shared the keyboard parts between them. It was strange to see my dad so passionate about the music, so determined they should perform the songs exactly right. He had ambitions, goals and dreams. This wasn't the Garry I knew at all. I admired his strong character, his urgency and perfectionism. I even began to like his sense of humour and laughed the loudest at his dry, spiteful remarks – most of them jibes at Welly.

Murph was quieter, more thoughtful, and probably more intelligent than Garry. He listened to Garry's plans for their domination of the music world with a wry smile, as if he knew that he was not going to make it to that particular party. If fame and fortune came Murph's way he wasn't going to turn it down, but it wasn't why he was bashing away at the drum skins for hour upon hour. He just liked playing. Everywhere he went he would beat out some new routine on the wardrobe, the banisters, the kitchen table – his fingers forever restless, his head nodding with satisfaction as he worked out exactly what he was going to do for such and such a section. He was a walking, talking drum kit, was Murph.

It was Friday afternoon. Murph and Garry had been into town to check out the venue for the Battle of the Bands and had returned to the house, bouncing with excitement.

"Look! We're on the poster!" enthused Garry. He unfurled a piece of large blue paper.

Mary Murphy peered at the long list of contestants. "They should have put you near the top. You nearly won it last year, didn't you?"

"It's in alphabetical order. That's why we're down there."

"Hmmm..." she murmured, unsatisfied by the explanation. "I'm making a shepherd's pie for tea. I suppose you'll want to stay?"

"Please!" said Garry instantly, but Shez shook her head.

"Now, I hope you're not on some diet, young lady." Mary Murphy wagged a finger and gave Shez a brief visual inspection. I wondered whether she had noticed the slight thickening around her tiny waist.

"No, I just can't eat much in this weather," Shez reassured her.

"Not nervous, are you?" enquired Murph as they climbed the stairs to his room.

"'Course not."

"You've been ever so quiet lately."

"I'm tired, that's all. I'll be fine on Saturday. Don't worry."

Shez sat on Murph's bed and rubbed her feet. She looked pale and hollow-eyed, weighed down by her secret.

"She's pregnant," I said out loud. But nobody heard.

"Charlie asked if he could borrow my big amp," said Garry. "What do you think, Shez? Should I say yes?"

"No, let him hire one in. It'll only get wrecked."

"It'll be all right as long as you keep an eye on it," reasoned Murph.

"Well, it's your lookout," Shez grimaced. "Anyway, how you going to get it there? You'll never get it on the bus."

"Charlie said he'd come and pick it up in his van in the morning."

"That's no good." Murph pulled off four small pieces of Blu-Tack and pressed them onto the corners of the poster. "We'll need it to practise in the afternoon."

"That's true... I'll tell him he can't have it till five."

"Not long to go now..." Murph picked up his drumsticks and crashed the cymbal. "Let's get started."

The three of them began to play "Don't Let Me Go". I was the private audience – so private that even the performers didn't know I was there. Murph was nodding, immersed in the rhythm, smiling as they moved smoothly from verse to chorus and back again. Garry

◀◀ 176

went into the solo, his fingers dancing up and down the neck of his guitar, his eyes sparkling, his mouth in a wide, triumphant grin. Shez picked out a simple bass-line and sang out above the music, clear and steady at first. But, as she started to listen to what she was saying, her voice faltered and her eyes filled with tears. This ordinary love song, addressed to nobody in particular and probably scribbled in the back of an exercise book during a boring lesson, had become a desperate plea from her unborn child. At least, that was how it sounded to me.

*I just want to stay with you, but you want to let
   me go.*
I just want to be with you, but you just tell me no.
*I can't stand this situation, my life's full of
   complication.*
*I just want to stay with you, but you want to let
   me go.*

Shez faltered and stopped. "I'm sorry," she whispered. "I can't sing today." She sat down on the bed, biting her lip, forcing back the tears.

"What's up?" said Garry, throwing down his guitar. Murph opened the window, and a blast of hot sticky air filled the room.

"I'm scared…"

"Of what?" Garry sat down and put his arm round Shez.

"Bad things are going to happen," she murmured.

"No, they're not. Good things are going to happen.

Great things. I promise. You wait till tomorrow." He wiped her tears with his fingers; kissed her neck, her hot, red cheeks, her raw, bitten lips.

Murph turned away, embarrassed. He stared at the Battle of the Bands poster, the top right-hand corner already peeling away from the wall. He reached up and pressed it back.

Suddenly the picture of Murph's headstone hurtled forward from the back of my memory, screeching to a halt in my mind's eye. I was consumed by a vision of spotless white marble: yellow-and-purple pansies at the base, fresh pink roses in a sunken vase, the smell of lemon cleaning fluid. My eye became a zoom lens, focusing on the inscription – small, gold lettering shining in a haze of sunshine. At last, I had been sent a message from the future:

In fondest memory of
Liam Murphy
Who left us 19 July 1986

July the nineteenth, that was the date on the poster. Murph was going to die on the day of the Battle of the Bands. Just like me.

17

The rest of the Stride practice was abandoned and Garry took Shez home. I was torn between going with them – in the hope that Shez would tell Garry about the baby – and staying with Murph. But this was supposedly Murph's last night on earth. I didn't want him to spend it alone, even if he didn't know I was with him.

Murph played the drums for a few minutes, then rested the sticks on the bass and lay on his bed. I sat on the floor and watched him as he put his hands behind his head and stared at the ceiling. He looked vaguely troubled. Was some serious problem nagging at him, or was he just trying to decide what song they should play for the first round of the competition tomorrow?

I tried to imagine how I would have felt if Weird Welly had told me that I was going to die at the Battle of the Bands. What would I have done with my last night? Got blind-drunk? Settled a few scores? Lost my virginity? I liked to think that I would have done *something* with those last few hours. Now Garry and Shez had gone, Murph had nothing much to do except watch the television with his mum.

Downstairs, Mary Murphy was having a last night, too – a last night of listening to the drums thumping through the ceiling, of trying to understand the grunting speech of teenage lads, of making shepherd's pie for more than one person. This was her last night of happiness, of sanity. After tomorrow she would have to resort to God for company – God and a few photos on the mantelpiece, random shots taken over the years that would now have to serve as documentary evidence of Murph's short life. A baby in a christening gown, a toddler making a sandcastle, a boy on a bicycle...

Who wants to know when they're going to die? Hardly anybody. It would be too overwhelming – the average person would be paralysed with fear. Of course, I had heard of brave kids with terminal illnesses who chose to spend their final weeks in Disneyland, and people with cancer who climbed mountains and ran marathons. But knowing that you're going to die soon is not the same as knowing you're going to die tomorrow. The only people who understand that are the criminals on Death Row. Even then, there is always the chance that their execution will be delayed at the last second. And what about people who kill themselves? They know as they pull the trigger or kick away the chair that this is their final moment. But then, they always have the power to stop – to put the gun away, untie the noose.

No, I concluded, the only certain death was a death that had already taken place. But maybe even that wasn't true – not if the Past, Present and Future kept careering around the universe, supposedly avoiding each other, yet in fact doing their best to collide. I remembered something that Weird Welly had said, a phrase I had found baffling at the time but which now made perfect sense. Will tomorrow happen because of yesterday, or did yesterday happen because of tomorrow? Here I was, with the twenty-twenty vision of hindsight. What if I could somehow get through to Murph and persuade him to stay indoors all day tomorrow – or at least not get in a car of any description? I got up and sat at the foot of his bed and began to talk.

"Murph," I whispered. "Murph, can you hear me? Please, try to listen. If you concentrate really hard, maybe you'll catch my voice. It's probably on some frequency that you're not used to – search the airwaves, Murph… It's Liam here… Another Liam… Please, try to listen. It's not a faint buzz on the amplifier or the wind in the garden or the sound of distant voices in the street – it's me. I have a message for you. Don't go to the Battle of the Bands tomorrow. Stay indoors. Get the flu, break your arm – just make an excuse… Murph? Can you hear me? Stay away."

There wasn't a quiver of a reply, not a twitch of recognition, not a momentary furrowing of the forehead. He remained motionless, staring at the poly-styrene tiles on his ceiling, as if a few white squares held the key to his future, rather than me. I looked up and studied the white frosty swirls, the imperfect matching of horizontal and vertical lines. And there I saw it. Etched into the tile directly above his pillow, with a penknife, perhaps, or a razor blade, and so small it was hardly visible, was a single word. A name – "Sheryl".

"Now I know what you would do with your last night, Murph," I said. "You would spend it with her."

So Murph was in love with Shez. But Shez was in love with Garry, although not so much in love that she wanted to keep his child. My discovery had instantly complicated the situation. I tried to think of all the alternative outcomes – it was like a wretched maths problem. What if ... Shez doesn't have the abortion, marries Garry, Murph dies – nothing changes. Shez has the abortion but still marries Garry – pointless. Shez has the abortion, splits up with Garry, Murph doesn't die and ends up with Shez – happy ever after for them but disastrous for me. And those weren't the only possibilities.

One thing was certain – even if I could alter the events of tomorrow, there was no way I could control the next sixteen years. Those wheels were turning fast and, now I'd started meddling with Time, I had to carry on. But I couldn't do it without Welly's help. So later that evening, I slipped through the back door as Mary Murphy was putting out the rubbish and made my way to his house.

Luckily, Welly was sitting in the back garden, a patchwork blanket over his knees like some old-age pensioner. He was sipping a cup of hot tea and nibbling weakly at a chocolate biscuit. I hadn't bothered him for three whole days. No doubt he believed that the anti-depressants were taking effect and he was on the road to recovery. How wrong he was.

I jumped over the garden fence and landed in front of him on the grass. "Hi, Welly!" I said. "I'm back."

"You!" he spluttered, spilling tea onto his lap. "You do not exist. You are not here. You do not exist. You are not here," he chanted mechanically.

"Come on, Welly, you don't believe that shit. You know full well that I'm real."

"You do not exist! Stop it! Go away!" He put his hands over his ears and made for the kitchen door. The blanket wrapped itself around his ankles and refused to be kicked free. A small hole in the centre of a turquoise patch caught on the buckles on his shoes, tripping him up and sending him flying into a pot of newly planted geraniums. Welly sat amid the floppy green leaves and the dark, crumbly earth, pounding the patio with childish frustration. A small red petal landed on his knee like a bloody graze.

"You can't escape me, Welly. Just accept it," I said calmly.

"Leave me alone!"

"I will, but first you must help me."

Welly pulled the blanket over his head and became a trembling mound of multicoloured woolly squares. "OK … OK … I'm sure this is still all inside my head, but if it gets rid of you, I'll do it… I'll do anything."

"I've remembered when Murph is meant to die – it's tomorrow."

"At the Battle of the Bands?" he asked in a dull, muffled voice.

"Well, the same day, anyway. Now, Charlie – I think he's the guy that I know, who runs Scurvy Joe's – I think he's going round to Murph's house tomorrow to pick up an amp – at about five."

"Charlie hasn't got a car. Only a transit van."

"Car, van, what's the difference? You told me it was a car crash. That doesn't mean it couldn't have been in a van," I said impatiently.

"I never told you – you told me."

"No, you told me – oh, forget it… Just find a way to stop him getting into the van."

"And that's it?"

"Well, yes," I replied. "But you'll have to keep an eye on him until midnight. Just in case someone offers him a lift somewhere or he gets a taxi home."

"It's not going to work," he moaned.

"Well, it'd better, or I shall haunt you for the rest of your life and you'll end up in some padded cell wearing a straitjacket."

"I hate you," Welly said vehemently.

"And you're a pain in the arse," I replied. "You might as well know the truth about your future. You don't run a music shop, just a crummy junk shop full of old mattresses and gas cookers. Everybody thinks you're a bit of a crank. You're not married – you don't have girlfriends; as far as I know, I was your only friend. Your hair is long and greasy, you stink of joss sticks, you've got metal studs in your face and you fancy yourself as a bit of a wizard. 'Weird Welly', that's what you're known as. You're into black magic – you perform rituals in graveyards. You've even been arrested for dancing round trees without any clothes on."

Welly put down the wilting plant and sat back down in the spilt earth. A troupe of ants carrying a large chocolate-biscuit crumb made a diversion and moved round him. He squinted at me, as if hoping I was no more than a trick of the light. "I'm really ill, aren't I," he said, after a long pause. "You're a manifestation of my fear and anxieties. That's what the doctor said. That means I'm going mad."

"No, you're not," I insisted. "But don't try to puzzle it out. Just save Murph. What have you got to lose?"

"Just my mind," he grunted.

"Who knows?" I replied. "Save his life, and Murph might let you back into the band. One good turn deserves another."

At that moment, his mum popped her head round the kitchen door. "Pete! Get off that damp concrete," she called. "You're due for your next dose of tablets."

I was still left with the problem of my own Future, or my Past – or my Present, come to think of it. Everything had become tangled like a knot in a wet shoelace. Welly didn't have a chance in hell of convincing Shez to keep her baby. So what was I to do? Be patient, I told myself, take one step at a time. But it didn't stop me roaming the streets, desperately searching for her and Garry. I felt that if I could at least overhear their conversation, it might put my mind at rest. There were plenty of places to go if you wanted to have a heart-to-heart, and I thought I knew most of them. But I didn't find them in the Grenadier or the Coach and Horses. They weren't weeping over a cheeseburger in McDonald's or embracing over a bucket of Kentucky Fried Chicken. I checked bus shelters and park benches. I walked along the towpath of the cut and crept through the dark, dripping tunnel that runs under the railway line. A train thundered overhead. Where were they? Not Rough Wood, surely? But I'd tried everywhere else.

Rough Wood was a nasty patch of woodland full of half-made dens and abandoned bonfires. It was where kids always ran away to after a bad row at home but never stayed longer than about half an hour. The tree trunks were scorched and scarred, their pathetic foliage choking on the fumes from the nearby motorway that droned in the background. Only in late spring did the bluebells triumph, pushing their way up between the chip wrappers and crushed cans, carpeting the ground in a defiant purple that even the hardest thug stopped to wonder at. But it was summertime now, and the bluebells had long since died.

I picked my way along the vague paths of trodden-down weeds. In the middle of the wood was a man-made clearing, its centrepiece a burnt-out car – how it had got there was a mystery. The shell was full of stinking rubbish – foil containers from Chinese takeaways, empty bottles of cider, fag ends and old tubs of Evo-stick. Its rusty floor was covered in countless plastic bags, twisted with dried glue. It wasn't pleasant here, but it was relatively harmless compared to *my* version of Rough Wood. The glue-sniffing had long since been replaced by proper drugs – the burnt-out car was now littered with used syringes and charred pieces of silver foil. But all I saw that evening was a couple of ten-year-olds sharing a cigarette.

I sat down on a rotting car seat and thought about the Future. There I was with all this information about my family. I knew who was going to marry whom, the names of their kids, where they would work, who would give them the sack, when they were going to die. But I didn't like having all this knowledge. It stank.

Being a dead teenager was far more stressful than being a living one, even though nobody tried to make you get up in the morning or moaned at you about the state of your bedroom. I had no control, no influence – no impact on anything. When I stood up I wouldn't leave even a moment's impression of my bum on the seat.

I left Rough Wood and made my way back to Welly's house, taking up guard in the front garden. I was feeling tired and weak, and wondered whether I was due for another spell in Dark Oblivion. It would be just my luck, I thought, to black out and disappear at the vital moment. I lay down on the wet, dewy grass. During the long hours of darkness I felt powerless and defeated. But when the morning sun washed over the front of Welly's house and sneaked through a gap between his bedroom curtains, a feeling of hope rushed through me – a naïve, groundless hope –

the kind you get when the lottery balls spin around the drum. I felt as if I'd bought a ticket for the National Lottery and put my mark through Welly's name. It was more than likely that he would fail me, but on this bright, sunny Saturday morning I would go against the odds.

18

"Come on, Welly! Wake up!" I shouted at his window. Either he was fast asleep or he was ignoring me. "I'm waiting for you!" I screamed. There was still no reply. I paced up and down the front lawn, shouting his name every few seconds. I was not at full strength, and this was a waste of my sapping energy. July the nineteenth had begun eight hours ago. Murph could already be dead for all I knew. Perhaps he had gone out and caught a taxi home at two o'clock in the morning. Perhaps he went for a bike ride at 5 a.m. and was run over by the milkman. All sorts of things could have happened while Welly slept.

I finally spotted him at eleven o'clock, in the lounge, sitting in front of Saturday morning television. He was still in his pyjamas and idly munching his way through a bacon sandwich. I pressed my face against the window and hollered through the glass.

"What the hell do you think you're playing at?" I shouted. "Get dressed and get out here, now!"

He paused for a few seconds between bites – a pause

that told me he could definitely hear me. But he didn't turn his head, just kept his eyes resolutely on the screen. "I'm warning you, Welly. I can make your life hell if I have to." I didn't know how exactly, but I'd find a way.

Welly licked the bacon fat from his fingers and wiped his hands on his dressing gown. Then he calmly got up and left the room. I ran round to the back garden but I couldn't see him. Maybe he was upstairs, getting dressed as I had told him to, but, then again, he could have gone back to bed. I desperately needed to get inside the house. Time was ticking.

All my early-morning optimism faded like the sun, which was now sulking behind a large, grey cloud. I was about to abandon Welly and try my luck at Murph's, when he walked out of the front door, washed, dressed and hair-gelled.

"You took your time," I grumbled. "I was just about to devise your first torture... Come on, then, what's your excuse?"

"Not here," he hissed. "If Mum sees me talking to thin air again, she's going to have me put away."

"We'd better get out of here quick, then... First stop, Murph's."

As we walked up to the house, I felt a wave of relief. Stride were practising, the drums signalling that Murph was still very much alive. Shez was singing and Garry was on guitar. It was as if everything was back to normal. She didn't tell him last night, I thought to myself, she can't have.

"Now what?" said Welly. "You're not expecting me to knock on the door, are you? Excuse me, Mrs

Murphy, I've come to save Murph's life?"

"No, no, of course not... Be quiet, will you? I'm thinking..."

"I thought you had a plan."

"I do – of sorts. We have to wait here until Charlie turns up for the amp. If Murph starts to get in the van, you have to stop him."

"Like how?"

"I don't know!" My head was spinning – the outer areas of my vision were darkening, like the edges of burning paper. I was starting to fade away. "Not now," I murmured. "Not now..." I fought for consciousness, clung onto the air with empty fists, but a stronger force was pushing me to the ground. "Don't let me down, Welly!" I shouted. And then it all went black.

This time I was aware of the Dark Oblivion. I was tossed through space like a piece of litter in a storm; hurled against a black wall that had no edges; thrown to the floor and then picked up again by an invisible hand. I swung in midair for a few moments, only to be thrown down again, this time into a deep well of nothingness. Falling, falling at great speed, head first – afraid of hitting the ground and yet wanting the fall to end. And just as I felt that I could bear the uncertainty no longer, a cold stream flooded through my veins and I was lifted up again. Now I was falling upwards into an endless sky. Up and up, feet first, my head swaying from side to side as I gasped at the deep blackness beneath me, above me, all around me – just nothing ... nothing.

And then it was over. I was back outside Murph's house. I felt as if I had only been away for a few seconds, but hours had passed – possibly even days. The place was silent. Nobody was in, and I had lost Welly. I ran along the street shouting his name.

"What day is it?" I asked an elderly woman pushing a Zimmer frame across the road. "What day? I need to know!" I raced down the hill towards the petrol station and slipped into the shop behind a fat trucker in a large checked shirt. I quickly scanned the few remaining newspapers on the rack. There was the *Pink*, a Saturday evening edition of the *Corsfield Mail* that contained all the sports results – it was still 19 July. Outside, the sky was still blue, but the sun was hanging low. "What's the time?" I shouted despairingly. "Isn't there a clock in here?"

The trucker picked up his chewing gum and a packet of crisps. "Put these on the petrol receipt, will you?" he said to the assistant behind the counter.

I craned my neck to look at the watch round his fat, hairy wrist, but the numbers were hidden under his sleeve. "I need to know the time!" I yelled, running around the tiny shop. "Somebody tell me the frigging time!"

I left the garage and carried on walking towards town. The shops were closed, the streets virtually empty. I walked towards the library, hoping against hope that the clock on the museum tower would be working. To my amazement, it was. The time was ten past nine. The Battle of the Bands was already in full swing. I ran all the way to Scurvy Joe's, or rather, the Shamrock Inn. Had it already happened? I was desperate to find out.

*   *   *

It felt strange to enter the scene of my own death – the same long, narrow room with the low ceiling. The bands had been set up at the far end, in front of an old fireplace. It was as if everyone had been invited to an eighties party but hadn't quite got the costume right. Nobody looked extreme enough. True, their jeans were narrower, their haircuts sharper, their glass lenses rounder, and they weren't all wearing trainers. But behind all that, they looked like the same bunch of mates I'd left behind. I scoured the room for familiar faces, my heart in my mouth. I recognized Garry's amp on the stage – it had obviously made it to the venue safely, but what about Murph?

I knew Garry would not be far away from his precious equipment and, sure enough, there he was, leaning against the corner of the bar, his gaze frequently drifting to the stage. Shez was standing next to him, her sparkly painted fingernails circled round a beer glass. Pregnant and drinking alcohol, was my first thought. But then, if she was still going ahead with the abortion, why shouldn't she poison her bloodstream? I felt like an undercover detective, mingling invisibly with the crowd, looking for the tiniest of clues. Garry was joking with a couple of mates, his free hand idly stroking Shez's back. I saw her stiffen slightly. Then Garry threw back his head and laughed in a gesture I had seen so many times before. It was the laugh he used when he was mocking some-body. I noticed that Shez didn't join in.

But where was Murph? Surely he was still alive. This wasn't how your friends behaved when you'd only just been killed – unless they didn't know – unless they were waiting for him. It was torture – knowing everything and yet knowing nothing. And more to the point, where the hell was Welly?

"Listen up! Listen up!"

Charlie had grabbed the mic and was trying to attract the crowd's attention.

It was the same Charlie that had hosted my Battle of the Bands – just thinner, hairier and younger-looking. "The judges have picked the final round line-up. Just three bands now, everyone, so listen up, will you? It could be you. I'm not repeating myself, so shut it!"

If anything, the buzz in the room got louder. He heaved a loud, weary sigh and shouted at the technician to turn the microphone up. "In alphabetical order ... it's Dark Horses ... Mind Games ... and Stride." There was a definite cheer when Charlie shouted the last name. I wondered briefly whether Salamander would have made it to the final three, whether we might even have won. But that was history – or the future, depending on how you looked at it. I had to forget all about that and concentrate on what was happening here and now. I suddenly realized that I wasn't in the Past at all – I was in the Present.

"We're on last," I heard Murph say, pushing his way towards Garry and Shez. He was alive – of course, he was alive. I knew that it had to be so, but it was still a relief to see him in the flesh.

"I think we should play 'Two-Faced' first and then 'Don't Let Me Go'," he said. "What do you reckon?"

"It's our best song – we always said we'd leave it till

last," said Garry. "How do you feel, Shez? It seemed to upset you last time you sang it. God knows why."

"I'll be all right," she replied.

"Sure?" asked Murph.

"Sure."

I managed to glance at Garry's watch. It was five to eleven. One hour and five minutes, during which Murph would somehow get into a car and drive off to his death. A lift home from a drunken friend seemed the most likely possibility – not that many of these kids were old enough to drive. Would it be a taxi, then? Or Charlie, taking the amp back to Murph's house? I needed Welly. The git had stood me up again. He must have rubbed his hands with delight when I faded away, skipping off back to his mother's clutches, his patchwork blanket, his cups of sweet tea. God, I hated him – even more than he hated me.

The finalists were allowed to perform two songs each. There was a fifteen-minute interval, which stretched to twenty while people faffed about adjusting the sound levels, altering the mics and retuning their guitars. Nobody seemed to mind – it gave the lads a chance to fight their way to the bar, and the girls enough time to queue for the toilet. But the waiting was agony for me. Murph stayed where he was, talking to Garry and Shez. He seemed calm, quietly confident. I took a last snapshot of them for my memory – three mates together. Friends and yet not friends. They had hidden desires, hopeless dreams – secrets. I was Shez's secret. If only she knew how much I loved her, I thought, as I watched her nodding absent-mindedly to the music, fiddling with the chain around her neck. Sparkly fingernails, and toenails, too, no doubt. That was my mum. I had tried to hate her over the past few days; God only knows she had given me enough cause. But I just couldn't. I couldn't believe that she didn't want me – I wasn't going to believe it.

"Come on, it's us," said Garry, bringing me back to the moment. He leapt onto the tiny stage and started to reset the levels on his amplifier.

"Best of luck, Shez," whispered Murph. "We can do it." He leant forward and planted a delicate kiss on her cheek.

"Don't," she replied sharply, shoving past him.

Murph stared after her as she went up to the microphone and pulled it down to mouth level.

"Come on, Murph!" Garry shouted.

The crowd was pressing forwards. A few of their supporters set up a chant: "Stride, Stride, Stride!" Garry grinned and waved as he plugged in his guitar. Murph lowered his drum stool and took his drumsticks out of his back pocket. He raised them in the air.

"One–two–three–four…"

"Two-Faced" wasn't my favourite song of theirs. It was too hard-edged, too brittle. But I could see why they had chosen to play it. Murph had a short but impressive drum solo, and Garry's guitar work was flashy and complicated. The three judges, who were sitting on a small raised platform at the back of the room, scribbled notes and beat time with their pencils. They were two guys from local music venues and the boss of Rocking Records, a small record label based in Wolverhampton.

Garry briefly took over Shez's spot in front of the

microphone. "Our last song was written by Murph –
that's our drummer, in case you don't know." Murph
played a roll and bashed his cymbals accordingly. The
crowd cheered.

"It's the only song of ours he's ever written, but it's
our best. At least, that's what I think. It's called 'Don't
Let Me Go'." There were more cheers, whoops and
applause. Murph did a count-in with his sticks; Garry
came in with his familiar guitar intro; Shez moved her
mouth close to the microphone and began to sing.

*I just want to stay with you, but you want to let
    me go.*
I just want to be with you, but you just tell me no.
*I can't stand this situation, my life's full of
    complication.*
*I just want to stay with you, but you want to let
    me go.*

The song wasn't about me – of course, it wasn't about
me. Murph had written it for Shez. He was in love with
her, but she had turned him down.

Don't let me go, like a fish on a hook,
You're throwing me back, without a second look.

Shez was trembling, her thin body swaying gently from
side to side, as if she was on a ship in a storm and
couldn't find her balance. The crowd swayed from side
to side, waving their arms in a single movement, like a
beast with a thousand heads. Shez had a glazed look in

her eyes. Everything swam before her as she grabbed hold of the microphone stand for support.

Give me a chance to prove that I can be the one.
Don't tell me that it's over when—

Suddenly, she jerked backwards, her eyes rolling up into her head. The guitar dropped from her hands and crashed to the floor. I instinctively jumped onto the stage and tried to catch her, but she slipped through my invisible fingers and fell into Garry's arms instead.

"What's wrong?" cried Murph, leaping from his stool and rushing across to her side.

"She's fainted," said Garry. He lifted Shez up in his arms and pushed his way out of the side door. It was dark now, and the street was almost empty. Garry laid Shez gently on the pavement, resting her head on his knees. Murph was close behind, carrying the glass of water he always kept behind his drum stool.

"Here, splash a bit on her face," he said. As Garry dipped his fingers in the water, I glimpsed the time on his watch. It was quarter to twelve.

19

"Still alive, then?" said a slurred voice out of the darkness. Welly staggered out of a shop doorway. He looked terrible. His hair was plastered over his head like he had soaked it in water, his eyes were staring wildly and his mouth was slopped open. A can of beer swung loosely in his hand. He had splashes of vomit down his shirt.

"Welly!" I shouted. "Where have you been? What the hell have you been doing?" I ran up to him and was instantly knocked back by the overpowering smell of glue.

"Yeah, I bin sniffing glue ... and lager... Not sniffing lager, drinking it." He giggled. "And I've taken my tablets, like the doc said... But it don't make no difference ... what I take ... 'cos YOU – YOU are still here!"

"Is he talking to us?" whispered Murph.

"Don't know, don't care," Garry replied in a louder voice. "I might have known he'd turn up. Trying to cause trouble. Get rid of him, will you?"

"I'll try."

Shez opened her eyes and lifted her head.

"You OK, Shez?" said Garry tenderly.

"Did we get to the end?" she murmured.

"Kind of," he replied. "They're doing the judging now... Here, drink this."

"I'm sorry..."

"Shh..."

Murph went up to Welly and tried to take him by the arm. "Come on," he said. "I'll find you a taxi."

"No!" shouted Welly suddenly. "No taxis! No cars, no vans... Those are my orders. From HIM!" He pointed at me with a trembling finger. "You, Murph, you ... should be ... dead by now, mate. Dead."

"No, you should," barked Garry. "Piss off."

Welly laughed and shook his head.

"Can't ... piss off ... not allowed ... to ... piss ... off. Got to stay ... save his life. That's what HE said. Him there... One good turn deserves another, eh?"

"I don't know what you're going on about. Just leave us alone, will you!" cried Murph. "Can't you see Shez's not well?"

"Nah, she's all right – just pregnant. Pregnant's not ill..."

"What did you say?"

Garry turned angrily towards Welly. "What did you say?"

"Hasn't she told you?" Welly folded over in a fit of giggles. "You see, I know things you don't. Know all sorts ... of things ... about you. About all of you."

"Do you want this in your face?" Garry shifted his knees from Shez's head and stood up, raising his fist.

"She's not pregnant, OK?"

"You ask her... Go on, ask her."

"I don't have to ask her!"

"No?" Welly pointed at Shez, who had curled up into a tight ball.

"Is it true?" whispered Murph, putting his arms around her. "Shez, tell me, is it true?"

She nodded and broke into loud, heaving sobs.

"But it can't be," insisted Garry. "Can't be... You wouldn't let me... We had to wait, you said..." He stopped short and looked at the two of them, hugging each other, rocking back and forth. There was a moment of stillness, of realization. He was a man in the middle of an earthquake. Within a few seconds his whole world had collapsed, leaving him standing amid the ruins, dazed and only just comprehending.

"I'm sorry," Shez mumbled, not daring to raise her head.

Welly burst into hysterical laughter, staggered over to the side of the pavement and threw up.

"Now that's something even YOU didn't know!" he jeered at me, a long run of yellow spittle dripping from his chin.

"Then who?" I shouted. "Who is my father?"

"You bastard..." Garry stared down at the two of them. "You bastard..."

"Why didn't you tell me?" Murph's voice cracked.

Shez lifted her face. Her black eyes shone in the darkness. "I'm sorry," she mumbled. "I'm so sorry."

Garry wasn't my father; Murph was – the drummer that nobody spoke about. Garry was nothing to do with me. I had Murph's genes, Murph's flesh and blood. I even had his name.

"How long has this been going on, then?" Garry thundered. "How long have you been screwing each other behind my back?"

"It wasn't like that," pleaded Murph. "It only happened once."

"Oh, so that makes it all right, then, does it?"

"I mean, it wasn't planned, we didn't – oh God, I can't believe you're pregnant, Shez – oh, shit... Oh, God... What are we going to do?"

"She's getting rid of it," chipped in Welly as he spat the last of the vomit onto the pavement and wiped his mouth on his shirt.

"How come he knows what's going on and nobody else does?" screamed Garry. "What is it, you going with him, too, Shez?"

"Shut up! No, no, 'course I'm not..."

"I wouldn't have her if she jumped on me," snarled Welly. "Tart."

"Shez, you can't get rid of it!" said Murph, grabbing her by the shoulders.

"I was going to tell you, both of you, but – but –" she stuttered, "the band – you so wanted to do this thing, and I thought if – if I just had the abortion and didn't tell anyone – I thought –"

"You thought what?" screamed Garry. "That you could treat me like shit and it'd be all right 'cos I'd never find out?"

Shez backed away from him – she looked scared.

"You can't have an abortion, Shez," begged Murph.

"You can't. I'm a Catholic, Shez – my mum's a Catholic... It's my baby too and you can't..."

"Oh, shut up, will you?" roared Garry. He grabbed Murph by his T-shirt and threw him against the wall. "You ... you were supposed to be my best mate..." He drew back his hand and thumped Murph in the face. Murph's head bounced off the brickwork. Then he lurched forwards and pushed Garry away. He stumbled backwards and tripped over Shez, who was still crouching on the pavement.

"Stop it," she cried. "Just stop it!"

Murph's and Garry's eyes met, and then they lunged at each other, fists flying through the air, kicking and pushing, grunting and crying. Soon there was blood streaming from Garry's nose and he was cut above his left eye.

"Somebody stop them!" yelled Shez. She staggered to her feet and tried to get in Garry's way, but he shoved her to one side and landed a punch on Murph's mouth. His lip started to bleed. They stood back from each other for a couple of seconds, breathing heavily, wiping the sweat from their faces. Then they charged at each other again, Murph locking his arms around Garry's waist in a desperate embrace. Garry tore him free and kicked him to the ground. Murph's drumsticks fell out of his pocket and rolled into the gutter, but he scrambled to his feet.

I watched dumbfounded as they struggled and pulled and grabbed. The man I'd always thought was my father was fighting the man who actually *was* my father. And strangely, in those terrifying moments when I thought they would kill each other, I loved them both. Was this what had happened on the night that nobody would talk about? Or had Welly and I changed everything? What was different; what was the same? There I was, with all my knowledge of the Future, and suddenly I didn't know anything at all.

Garry and Murph wrestled each other off the pavement and into the road. They were swinging wildly, tearing at each other's clothes, clinging onto each other and then pushing away. Years of love had been forgotten in a few moments of hate. They weren't fighting over Shez and her unborn child. This was about the two of them and nobody else. It was a dark world that they had entered, and they were oblivious to everything around them. Shez was screaming at the roadside, begging the two of them to stop. Welly had sunk into a stupor against the wall. He poured the remains of his lager over his head and laughed like some demented goblin. He had finally gone weird.

By now, several people had streamed out of the pub and were standing on the pavement. Voices shot out of the darkness.

"What are they fighting about?"

"Somebody call the police!"

"You're meant to be on stage! Everyone's waiting for you!"

"You've won!"

Garry stopped, his fist raised in the air. He looked up for a moment and Murph socked him full in the face. Garry went flying backwards and hit his head on the kerb. He lay there, motionless, blood still pouring from his nose and down his neck. A few people ran to his side. Murph stood in the middle of the road, panting heavily. He put his hand through his hair in a gesture of disbelief. There was silence. And then sounds … a series of distinct sounds … the roar of a car careering round the corner, a sudden screech of brakes, a swerve, gasps, screams. And then silence again.

I saw Murph's body being thrown upwards, spinning in the air like a leaf. For a few seconds he seemed to be flying through the darkness in slow motion, then suddenly he flopped down, thudding onto the bonnet before he rolled under the front wheels. The car ran right over him and crashed into a telephone box.

"He's dead," said Welly, crushing the can of lager in his palm. "I know he's dead."

Murph was sprawled on his back, one leg twisted over the edge of the kerb, his head in the gutter. He was very still. Garry lay a few feet away from him, bloody and unconscious but still breathing. The driver of the car pushed open his door and staggered out, dazed and disorientated, as if he had just crash-landed on another planet. A few people were bending over the two bodies – somebody shouted that an ambulance was on its way.

Most of the crowd had backed off, and people were huddling against the wall, their arms round each other, their mouths open in disbelief. A girl was sick. Others started to bawl. Shez was still standing on the edge of the pavement. She hadn't even moved to get away from the car. She was paralysed with shock.

I bent down and picked up the drumsticks. Yes, I could pick them up, feel them and turn them over in my hand. Something in the universe had changed. I walked up to Murph. The small crowd parted for me, as if they sensed I was there. Murph's eyes flickered open and he looked at me. It was a brief gaze, a moment of recognition. I knelt down and touched his hand. I could feel his cold, sweating skin; could grasp his fingers in mine.

"I'm Liam," I began.

I had a thousand things to say. But there was no time. I could hear a siren whining in the distance, the sound moving ever closer.

Murph nodded slightly then closed his eyes and died.

I took his hand and gently pulled him upwards. His spirit left his body with a wrenching sigh. We left the scene behind – girls wailing; boys sobbing; Shez with somebody's jacket round her shoulders, still rooted to the spot; the driver leaning over his damaged bonnet, shaking his head in disbelief; two ambulances side by side, blocking the street, blue lights flashing in the darkness; paramedics in fluorescent waistcoats; stretchers, drips, blankets; Garry being lifted on board and whisked away; a queue of cars held up by a policeman on a motorbike; another policeman unrolling a strip of red-and-white tape across the road. They all became smaller and smaller, until they were nothing but dots in the distance below. Upwards we flew, upwards into the darkness – just the two of us, Murph and me. We didn't speak or even look at each other. We just drifted...

fast-forward ▶▶

20

"His eyes are open!" A woman's voice – the scrape of a chair.

"My God! I'll call the nurse." A man's voice this time, two people in the room, a buzzing noise.

Two blurred faces peering into mine. Two smiles. An embrace. Brief laughter. Tears.

Footsteps. The buzzing sound stops.

"Something the matter?"

"He's woken up!"

Another face. I don't recognize the features – a crisp, white dress, the smell of lavender. My arm is held up; something is wrapped around it, squeezes it tight, then releases. I feel the corners of my mouth lifting.

"He's smiling," says the man. "Look, he's smiling."

The back of my head is tender. I want to touch it but I can't lift my hand. I'm not even sure where my hands are. My brain searches for a few moments then gives up. My limbs feel disconnected.

"Liam, love, can you hear me? Do you think he can hear me?"

Yes, Mum, I can hear you. I nod my head, very slightly. It hurts.

"He nodded his head. He understands!" says Garry. They embrace. More tears. I close my eyes.

That was, as they say, the First Day of the Rest of My Life.

I was not dead. I was assured that I had never been dead, although they had "nearly lost me" several times. It was mid-February. For nine weeks I had lain in a deep coma, while God, or whoever was in charge of these things, umm-ed and aah-ed about whether to keep me or let me go. In the end He probably decided that I was more trouble than I was worth, let me off the hook and threw me back in the water.

After a few days, I was allowed to sit up. My room was small and square with pale yellow walls. A large chequered window looked out into a dark corridor. Unfamiliar faces glanced at me as they walked by – doctors, nurses and people visiting other patients. Children pressed their noses against the glass and were pulled away. I turned my head and stared through the window on the opposite wall. As far as I knew, the outside world was the precise shape of a rectangle, about one and a half metres wide and a metre high. Anything could have been beyond the edges of the frame. All I could see was an expanse of blue-tinged snow, the sun shining in a clear sky, white branches dripping. Somebody had built a snowman and put a stethoscope round its neck. A few lines of neat footprints led to and from a birdfeeder that had been hung on a nearby tree.

I watched the birds pecking at the nuts – were they sparrows, chaffinches, blue tits? The only bird I could name for certain was a robin, but no robins came. The snow was melting. I could see the frosty edges of paths and flower-beds gradually appearing, revealing an orderly garden. It was the same view, yet it changed almost constantly. I looked out of the window from early morning until dusk, trying to catch the blue sky deepening before the nurse drew my curtains and put the picture away.

Then I stared at the curtains themselves. I studied the smudgy yellow and orange flowers and worked out that the pattern repeated itself every ten centimetres. I turned my head to the front and wondered at the line of cuddly toys sitting on the shelf on the opposite wall. I saw that the shelf had not been hung completely straight, dipping slightly to the right. And there were other imperfections. On the ceiling, a tiny patch the size of a thick brush-stroke had not been repainted. There was a sweeping black mark on the grey tiled floor, where the door scraped. On the shiny brown surface of my bedside table I found a dent shaped like a heart.

I took an inventory of everything in the room. I counted the dull red grapes in my fruit bowl, the petals on a bright arrangement of flowers that were stuck into a square green sponge. I could describe every greeting card on my windowsill without looking at them, in order from left to right. First my birthday cards, with pictures of sketchy footballers and funky guitarists, then nativity scenes and jolly Santas stuck down chimneys, and finally a group of pastel teddies holding bunches of flowers that told me to "Get Well Soon", as if it were an order. In those early days it was enough just to look around the room and make mental lists of its contents, to stare outside and note the blades of grass emerging through the thaw. I was told that I was on the road to recovery, but I still wasn't convinced that I was alive at all.

"Everyone" had been to see me while I had been in the coma. Nan and Grandad, my dad's parents whom I hardly ever saw even though they only lived up the road, my auntie Jackie and uncle Rick, and Daz and CJ, of course. And Gemma had sat at my bedside so often she had finished knitting a long, multicoloured scarf, which she gave to me as a Get Well present. My visitors turned up without warning or invitation – I could guarantee that between the hours of two and four, and six and eight, I would never be alone. They picked at my fruit and flicked through my magazines. They had private conversations, made their plans for the weekend and told me news of people I had never heard of. "How are they treating you?" they asked. "What's the food like? Anything you want me to bring in?" The same questions again and again – it was driving me mad.

I was told countless times how "lucky" I was to be alive. If the ambulance hadn't arrived so quickly, if the head injuries department hadn't been one of the best in the country, who knows what might have happened? I didn't want to put a damper on everyone's fun, but I just couldn't share their enthusiasm. Strange, mind-blowing things had happened. My body may have lain in a hospital bed for nine weeks, but my spirit had been on the loose.

And who was my most regular visitor? Garry. True, he had more time on his hands than Mum, but it still surprised me when he turned up every afternoon with his newspaper. He read bits of sports news out to me while I stared out of the window and waited for the birds. Sometimes we played cards – blackjack and knockout whist. Mum came to see me every evening after work, often bringing Zoe. She held my hand and chatted on aimlessly about her day, while Zoe played with my radio headphones, flicking from channel to channel and singing along at the top of her voice until it was time to go home to bed.

One morning, my assigned nurse, Barbara, announced that I was being moved to a different room – because I was "doing so well". Various tests had been carried out and my future was looking bright. Barbara started to pack my few belongings. I watched her fold up my clean pyjamas and gather up my greetings cards. She swept the cuddly toys into her arms and laid them gently in a plastic box like babies in a cot. She put my toothbrush and toothpaste into a navy toilet bag I'd never seen before, folded up my flannel and rolled my towels. She opened my bedside drawer and took out two horror novels, neither of which I'd read, and a single cassette tape. It was the Stride demo.

"What's that doing here?" I asked, picking it up and turning it over in my hand. Barbara smiled and put her head on one side.

"Your mum and dad kept playing it to you while you were asleep," she said. "Over and over. It must be worn out. That your favourite band?"

"Sort of."

"That's what we do, you see," she continued breezily, as she put my flower vases and fruit bowl on the bottom of the trolley. "We get the family to play trauma patients their favourite pop music. And talk to them, of course. That's so important. It makes a huge difference. Sometimes a famous footballer can do the trick but, usually, all it takes is the sound of a familiar voice: Mum, Dad, girlfriend…"

"And did they talk to me?" I asked.

"Of course. You've probably got them to thank for your recovery. Sometimes we lose people and they never come back." She pushed the chinking trolley towards the door. "I'll just pop these over to your new room. Do you want the wheelchair or shall we try and manage without?"

I was too deep in thought to reply. Was the explanation so simple? During those weeks when I was hovering between life and death, Mum and Dad had told me about the past and I had dramatized their stories in my fevered, damaged brain. There had been no collisions of Time, no wandering through the spirit world. I had experienced nothing more than a series of vivid dreams. But if that were the case, then why had Weird Welly behaved as if he already knew me; why had he made all those dark hints about what was going to happen?

It wasn't going to be easy, but I had to talk to Mum

and Dad. That evening my nan and grandad turned up with a big box of chocolates, most of which they ate while they rambled on at me about nothing in particular. And the next day Gemma spent the entire afternoon trying to get me to do a jigsaw of some ponies in a field. "It's good brain exercise," she assured me, but I wasn't interested.

Three days passed before I managed to see Mum and Dad on my own. Zoe had gone to a party and they only had half an hour before they had to pick her up. Half an hour would have to do.

"When I was unconscious," I ventured, "what did you do?"

"Just talked to you," replied Garry.

"What about?"

"Oh, nothing much. This and that."

"Did you tell me about what happened? You know – with Murph?"

Garry looked at Shez and raised his eyebrows. She bit her lip.

"I don't know what you mean," she said.

I took a deep breath and said, "He was my real father, wasn't he?" I studied their faces, trying to work out which of them had told me, but they looked equally taken aback.

"Yes, he was," replied Garry finally, gripping Shez's hand. Tears welled up in her eyes.

"Sorry, Liam," she began, her voice trembling.

"It's all right, Mum, really. Please don't cry." I turned to Garry. "You knew I wasn't yours but you still married Mum?"

"Yeah, well, we sort of did it in Murph's honour," Garry said.

"It was a noble thing to do. To take on somebody else's child."

"Unfortunately, noble feelings don't always last," he mumbled. "When you're only seventeen, married with a kid and no job, well, all I'll say is, it wasn't easy."

"You did your best. It was my fault," said Mum. "All my fault."

"No, it wasn't," Garry insisted. "I probably would have made of mess of things anyway. I just wanted somebody else to blame."

"But we've come through that now." Mum gave me a brave smile. "Your accident put things in perspective, Liam. It's changed everything."

"I'm glad you told him the truth, Shez. We always said we'd tell him one day, but somehow—"

"But I didn't tell him," she interrupted. "Honest, I didn't."

"But you must have!"

She shook her head.

Garry frowned. "If neither of us told him, then who the hell did?"

I let them puzzle it over for the rest of the visit. I suppose I could have interrogated everyone that had come to see me during those past nine weeks, but I didn't need to. All would become clear when I talked to Welly. I was desperate to see him. What an incredible conversation we were going to have.

I tried to phone him from the hospital, but Directory Enquiries didn't have a number for Weird Welly's, and

I couldn't remember the shop's proper name. I begged CJ and Daz to go down there for me and give him a message, but they said he was a creep and I should forget about him.

Even Gemma, who was being mysteriously devoted to me, refused to help. "I talked it through with your mum and I'm afraid she said it was a really bad idea," she soothed. "We're only concerned for your health, you know."

21

A couple of weeks later I emerged triumphant, if a bit shaky, from St Mary's Hospital to a party that would have pleased royalty. There were balloons hanging from the windows and a large banner across the front of the house – *Welcome Home, Liam* it read in shaky red lettering. I was hugged, kissed and marvelled at. Everyone wanted to shake my hand or pat me on the back – I felt like a human lucky charm. Mum's sister Jacky gave me a file of newspaper cuttings about the accident. I had made the headlines in the *Corsfield Mail* several times: "Drummer boy's life dangles by a thread", "Local pop idol in death-trap disaster", "Our nine-week hell is over, says drummer's dad" and, lastly, "Scurvy Joe's loses licence".

"Poor Charlie," I muttered. "All because a stage light fell on my head."

"Poor Charlie, my arse," said Dad. "We're suing the brewery. The solicitor reckons we should get thousands."

The celebrations lasted all afternoon and well on into

the evening. Our tiny lounge was full to bursting with family, friends and neighbours I'd never even met before. I was led to the sofa, where I was duly visited by a queue of well-wishers – most of whom ruffled my hair and told me to "take it easy". There was a lot of beer drunk, a lot of laughter and plenty of loud music. I couldn't believe it – music playing in our house! Dad had gone out and bought an expensive hi-fi system on interest-free credit. There was also a new fridge-freezer in the kitchen, and Mum and Dad were even talking about getting a new car. And all this was on the promise of some whacking great compensation cheque, which I was clearly meant to be sharing. But the material world did not interest me much – I just wanted to see Welly.

"Guess what, Liam?" said CJ, towering over me with a can of beer in his hand. "Daz and I have swapped to Sound Technology. It's really good – you should try it. We're learning all about the music industry."

"Yeah," enthused Daz, bouncing onto the arm of the sofa and nearly kicking me in the stomach. "And Gemma's dad's been giving me piano lessons. He said if I keep practising, I can do Grade Three next year."

"I don't believe it!" I shouted above the din. "I thought Salamander would have split up by now."

"Not at all," replied CJ. "We've been working really hard, waiting for your return, mate."

"Gemma said that if we gave up, it would be like accepting you were going to die," Daz explained kindly.

"But we always knew you wouldn't run out on us," CJ added.

"And what about you and Gemma?"

"Oh, that's all over, but we're still friends." He looked across the room and raised his thumb at Gemma, who was handing out onion bhajis and cheese rolls. She took it as a sign that he wanted some and edged her way through the throng towards us.

"Isn't it great?" she smiled, while Daz and CJ emptied the plate. "All these people love you!"

"Nah," I replied. "They've just come for the free booze."

Gemma squeezed in beside me. CJ and Daz wandered off in search of another drink. We sat in silence for a few minutes, listening to the music and the hum of the conversation.

"So, you've split up with CJ, then?" I said eventually.

"Yes … I was only carrying on because I didn't want to be out of the band," she answered. "And because of you."

"What d'yer mean?" I said, knowing full well.

"It was always you I really liked," she whispered. "When I thought you were going to die, it made me realize how much you meant to me. I cried and cried."

"Well, some pretty weird things happened while I was unconscious. It sort of changed my life."

"I think it's had a huge impact on all of us," she said.

"Like how?"

"You know, it's made us realize that life is short – that you have to live in the present, seize the moment, treat every day as if it's your last… That kind of thing."

"Really?" I looked around the room. CJ and Daz were exploring the features of Garry's flash new music system. Mum was standing by the French windows, a glass of fizzy wine in her hand, laughing with a couple of friends from work.

"I can't wait till we start playing together again, can you?" said Gemma.

"It'll be strange," I answered. "I haven't played the drums in months."

"I found your drumsticks, by the way. I was going to give them to you in hospital but your mum thought it might upset you."

"Why on earth should it upset me?"

"I don't know… Do you want them now?"

I nodded. Gemma reached into a large velvet duffel bag and pulled them out – Murph's drumsticks, which had once seemed full of magical powers. I took them in my hands and twizzled them through my fingers.

"Thanks," I said warmly. "You don't know how important these are to me." I turned and kissed her. Her breath smelt of onion bhajis, but it didn't matter. I was "seizing the moment" and it felt good.

"Let's talk later," I said. "I need to see my dad."

"Fine," Gemma chirped, trying desperately to take our first kiss in her stride. "I'll see if your mum needs any help with anything." She smiled and eased herself off the sofa, dragging her hand lightly along my leg as she went. I watched her bobbing across the room, her long, brown wavy hair tied back with an orange flower. It was amazing the things that could be achieved while lying unconscious in a hospital bed. I had found out who my real father was, fixed my parents' ailing marriage, turned Garry from being a drunken lout into a reasonable human being, and had just acquired a rich, fit-looking girlfriend. I didn't need to travel back in time to change the world. I just had to lie down for a bit and nearly die.

I found Garry standing alone in the front garden – my dad and yet not my dad. He waved his can of beer. "The only one, promise," he said, gesturing at me to join him. "I'm giving up, you know…"

It was a bright afternoon, but the wind was cold. The street was virtually empty because everyone was crammed into our living room. I noticed a new piece of graffiti on the gate opposite, and that number 15 had been boarded up again, this time with metal grids across the doors and windows. There was the same amount of litter in the street, the same dogs were barking their heads off, and the mattress outside the house next door still hadn't been taken away by the council. It was dirty and tacky and rough. But God, it was good to be home.

"So," I said. "Tell me about Welly."

"What's there to tell? He's just a smackhead."

"It's important, Dad…"

Garry took a large sip and hesitated.

"I want the whole story."

"Yeah, all right, I'm just trying to think where to start…" He leant back against the wall. "I knew Pete Llewellyn from primary school – same year but different class. He was never a close friend… Murph and I thought he was a bit of a mummy's boy – he dressed smart, never wagged off school, did his homework. I think he was bullied a bit. Anyway, when he was about fifteen, he decided it was all going to change. He tried to hang around with the cool guys – he wanted us to think he was dangerous, you know, on the edge. He started calling himself Welly, boasted how he nicked money off his mum to buy fags. Pretty tame stuff, really. I don't know exactly when he started on the glue – it was a big thing in the early Eighties. I only tried it once myself, couldn't stand the smell. But the stuff was easy to get hold of – cheap too."

"So how come he joined Stride?"

"He heard we was looking for a keyboard player and begged us to give him a try. I was against it – I didn't trust him. But he had a decent keyboard and he knew how to play... Shez and Murph thought he deserved a chance. They were always softer than I was." Garry smiled to himself and looked into the middle distance, as if reliving a particular moment: a phrase, a look, an atmosphere...

"And how long was he with the band?"

"Only a few months. It was a disaster right from the start. I think he was only sniffing glue 'cos he thought it would impress us. But it was getting to him, you know, it was mucking up his head. He never turned up on time for practices. Once he even failed to make a gig."

"But he's playing on the demo tape, isn't he?"

"Yeah. Only by chance... It was the only decent recording of the band we made and that idiot had to be on it," he said. "That's the main reason your mum and I wouldn't play it. It wasn't how we wanted to remember Stride."

So Welly had lied to me. At least, his version of the story had been crucially different. He had told me they'd all been best friends. He behaved as if he'd been part of the band from the beginning. I needed to go back and rewind all our conversations, to see things from a different angle. I had to talk to him and get everything straightened out.

"What happened to him after Murph died?"

"He had some kind of breakdown, I think." Garry put the empty can on the windowsill. "We were all cut up pretty bad about it. But Welly went dead strange. Dropped out of the scene completely. I think he was in some mental hospital for a while."

"All because of Murph's death?"

Garry shrugged. "It might have had something to do with it. The trigger, you know. I didn't see him for years – I've no idea how he ended up running that shop. He was into some pretty strange stuff. We kept out of his way. Everyone did. I think he's schizophrenic or something... I dunno, there's something wrong with him, that's for sure."

"Strange how things turn out, isn't it?" I said wistfully. "Now I know the truth, I feel more like we're father and son than ever."

"Yeah ... me, too."

"It's not good to have secrets."

"Suppose you're right," Garry sighed, putting his arm round my bony shoulders. "Suppose you're right..."

22

I didn't sleep very well that night. It felt strange to be back in my own bed. I had grown used to the hard mattress; the cold, slippery floor; the smell of disinfectant in the hospital bathroom; pull-lights and red buttons and the sound of buzzers going off in the night. My room was too quiet, too private. There were no nurses popping their heads around the door to check that I was all right. I couldn't stop thinking about what Dad had told me about Welly. As the night dragged towards dawn, I rehearsed several speeches to Welly in my head. I didn't want to talk in riddles any more. I wanted to know.

I got up about six o'clock. The room was icy cold, but at least there was some carpet on the floor. I got dressed and crept downstairs. The place was a mess – nobody had bothered to clean up before going to bed. I picked my way through the abandoned paper plates covered with half-eaten sausage rolls and spicy chicken wings, screwed-up napkins and torn plastic cups. I gently patted a silver helium balloon, which was floating through the room like a lost soul, and poured myself a large glass of warm orange juice.

If I left the house now, it would be too early, but I knew I had to get out before Mum and Dad woke up. The doctors had told me not to go out on my own until I felt completely better, but I had had enough of waiting. There was still unfinished business to settle. I wrote a brief note telling Mum not to worry and left it by the kettle.

I felt oddly vulnerable as I slowly made my way through the empty streets. I could walk well enough, but I was definitely weak. By the time I reached the edge of the estate, my legs were feeling heavy and wobbly. I had to sit down at the bus stop to rest. Should I, could I, do this? The air was cold and my fingers had grown numb in my pockets. I thought of the stifling warmth of the hospital, the smallness of my room, the security of the daily routines. By now they would be having breakfast – a tiny white bowl of cornflakes, cold yellow toast, the orange or apple that I never ate, the thin strawberry yoghurt. It suddenly made me feel hungry. I bought a packet of crisps and caught the bus to the station.

I remembered that first morning when I found myself in 1986, walking down the hill from Corsfield, walking through the maze of narrow streets by the railway sidings. There was the old newsagent's where I saw the date on the paper, and the workshop opposite, now boarded up and empty. Welly's shop was on the corner, just ahead. He would still be asleep – he wasn't the type to be an early riser.

But the shop was shut. More than shut – it had closed down. Some expiry notice had been pasted on the window, some legal gobbledygook about something not being paid, or a lease terminating. I couldn't understand it. No forwarding address – no proud MOVED TO NEW PREMISES sign. Nothing. I peered through the large shop window from every angle. There was a small pile of mail lying on the mat, and all the black magic stuff had gone. But the junk was still there, the same stinking mattresses and broken garden furniture. Now it would take another house clearance guy to empty the shop. Welly had evaded me again.

I sat down on the kerb and cried. Large tears ran down my cheeks and I wiped them on my sleeve till it was wet through. I felt worn to the core – my legs ached, my whole body felt like cold jelly. Where could I find him? Who would know where he had gone? I thought of ringing CJ or Daz, even of calling Gemma. But they wouldn't know and probably wouldn't help me. No, they would come and carry me home, put my feet up on the sofa, make me a cup of tea, tell me to forget all about him. I would have to continue alone.

I walked slowly back towards the town centre, stopping every now and then to rest. People were on their way to work, kids in uniform were crowding onto the buses, shutters were being raised on shopfronts – everything was so normal it made me angry. The number 95 bus arrived and I stepped on. I didn't know why, or exactly where I was going. I dropped my fifty pence in the slot and sat down. The bus chugged up the hill to Corsfield. Somehow I felt that the answer might lie there. Maybe Welly's parents were still living in their house – they might know where he was living now. There was a slim chance that he'd even gone back home.

I got off at the bus stop and turned the corner into Welly's road. I wandered up and down, staring at the doors, trying to remember which house had been his, cursing that I hadn't noted the number. Everything looked different from how I remembered – the houses just weren't right. Some had lawns, but most had driveways – concrete slabs or small pink paving stones. Windows had been replaced, glass porches built, front walls removed, gates put in. I wasn't even sure that these were the same houses to begin with. My head was reeling. I felt sick. Soon a postman came trundling up the street. From a distance he looked just like CJ. I waved at him and shouted.

"Do a Mr and Mrs Llewellyn live in this road?" I asked.

He frowned at me. "Why do you want to know?"

"I'm a friend of their son," I explained breathlessly. "Only I haven't been here for years. I've forgotten the number of their house."

"Don't think I'm allowed to give out that kind of information," he said, sorting idly through his pile of letters. "But there's no post for any Llewellyns today, I can tell you that much..." He caught my fallen expression. "Sorry," he added.

"That's OK," I replied. "It was just an idea."

I left Welly's road – if it ever had been Welly's road – and trudged on, further up the hill. As I stopped to look back at the grey, grimy landscape below, I made a mental list of the places I would try. I would go to the Job Shop, the Neighbourhood Office, the pubs, the Salvation Army Hostel, the YMCA, all the local graveyards, the mental hospital... I would put adverts in the newspapers. I'd leave notes in phone boxes. I would even search for him in Rough Wood. But in my heart I knew that I would never see Welly again. He had faded on me as I had faded on him, disappearing inexplicably into thin air.

I turned round and walked to St Cedd's at the very top of the hill. It was still early, and the church was shut. The graveyard was as bleak and windswept as ever. A bush was doing its best to cheer up the landscape with a display of small yellow flowers on twiggy stems, but it was a lost cause. I walked from gravestone to gravestone, reading the names and dates – James Barfield, died May 1878; Hannah Chambers, aged 24; Elizabeth Wright, 1921–1932. These brief factual details were all that was left of these long-forgotten people. I wondered whether their spirits had risen from the dead; whether they were happy now, reunited with loved ones, living in heaven. After all I'd been through I still didn't know whether I believed in God.

I needed to go home and lie down, but there was one more thing I had to do while I was here: visit my father's grave. I stood in front of his headstone and read the inscription again. Liam Murphy – perhaps that should have been *my* name. If Murph had lived, who knows, Mum might have married him instead of Garry. I tried to imagine them together, to cut Garry out of the picture and replace him with a tall, gangly lad with light brown hair. But I couldn't make it look right –

I couldn't age Murph to fit with Mum, no matter how hard I tried. So many times I had wished for a different father, or no father at all. And now I had one. Only he was dead and no real use to me. I put Garry back in the mental picture, with Mum, Zoe and me. Garry was my dad and yet not my dad – that was OK. I could live with that kind of contradiction.

I suppose I must have sat in the graveyard most of the morning. The sun was up now and a gentle wind was ruffling the pansies at the foot of the headstone. I felt a kind of peace and couldn't find a reason to move away. I didn't admit it to myself, but I was waiting for her to come. At midday, give or take a few minutes, Mary Murphy would be here, in her beige raincoat and headscarf, carrying a bunch of fresh flowers and a cleaning cloth in her handbag. She did not let me down.

Mary Murphy was surprised to see me. She hadn't heard about my accident, not being enough in this world to read newspapers or watch television. She had assumed our friendship was over, that I had deserted her along with all the others.

"I'm sorry about that day," I said. "The last thing I wanted to do was upset you."

"Never mind," she said. "It's over now… You look pale, Liam. When did you come out of hospital?"

"Only yesterday," I admitted.

"You're not ready to go dashing about. You must take it easy. Why don't you come back to the house? I'll ring your parents, ask them to come and pick you up."

"Maybe…" I hesitated. "There's something I need to tell you first."

We stood before the headstone and I told her that Murph was my real father. I told her that he had loved Shez and wanted her to keep the baby. She stood trembling in the wind, like a pale thin twig. Tears fell as she took my arm to steady herself.

"Why did nobody tell me?" she said, her voice breaking.

I didn't know the real answer, so I had to make it up. Shez and Garry had wanted to spare her the shock, I said. They didn't want to spoil her image of him. They felt she had suffered enough.

"The Lord has forgiven my son," she declared. "And so do I."

We walked slowly back to the house. I swear there was a new lightness in her step, a lifting of her head, as if a burden had lain on her shoulders for many years and had just been taken away. As we approached her tiny terraced house, I felt that a weight was lifting from me, too, pulling away from my body and drifting up into the sky. There it was – a small grey cloud being pushed along by the wind. Soon it would be out of sight. Finding Welly didn't matter any more. The truth I'd been searching for had nothing to do with time travel or ghosts or changing the past. It was to do with the present, with real life; not just mine, but Mary Murphy's. She was my unfinished business. She, too, had been lied to, kept in the dark – maybe with the best of intentions, but it had been wrong. Both of us had a right to know the truth about what had happened back in that summer of 1986. And now we did.

*   *   *

There were no instant transformations. Mary didn't throw a party and dance the Irish jig. But as the weeks went by she started to smile more often, and to visit the grave less often. She bought a new raincoat and went back to playing bingo on Thursday nights. The Stride scrapbook was put away in the drawer, and a new one was begun for Salamander. She invited CJ, Daz and Gemma round to tea and took a photo of us outside the house. We decided we would put it on the front cover of our demo CD when we got round to recording one. Mary also took a picture of me on my own, standing next to the rosebush by the front bay window. She put it in a silver frame and placed it on the mantelpiece, next to the picture of Murph taken at the same age. There we were, father and son. I couldn't see any physical similarity between us. Shez's and Murph's genes had somehow conspired to keep the secret well hidden. But Mary would look from one photo to the other and insist that we had identical noses and the same "soft smile". She was mistaken, but I indulged her. She was my nan, after all.

Oh, and one more thing...

She gave me his drum kit.

KEEPER
Mal Peet

In a newspaper office, Paul Faustino, South America's top football writer, sits opposite the man they call El Gato – the Cat – the world's greatest goalkeeper. On the table between them stands the World Cup...

In the hours that follow, El Gato tells his incredible life story – how he, a poor logger's son, learns to become a World Cup-winning goalkeeper so good he is almost unbeatable. And the most remarkable part of this story is the man who teaches him – the mysterious Keeper, who haunts a football pitch at the heart of the claustrophobic forest.

This extraordinary, gripping tale pulses with the rhythms of football and the rainforest.

FIRST FRENCH KISS & OTHER TRAUMAS
Adam Bagdasarian

Share the moments of comic confusion and tender transformation that make up one boy's wild ride through childhood and adolescence.

Meet Will as he struggles up a godforsaken mountain with other miserable campers, tosses aside all scruples to get in with the cool kids at school, searches for the true path to romantic love or tries to live up to his father's impossibly high standards. Funny and affecting, these tales take you through all the ups and downs of growing up, visiting triumph, humiliation, love, loss, kissing – and laxatives – along the way.